DIZZY'S WOMAN

by the same author

ANNA'S BOOK
THE LION OF PESCARA

Dizzy's Woman

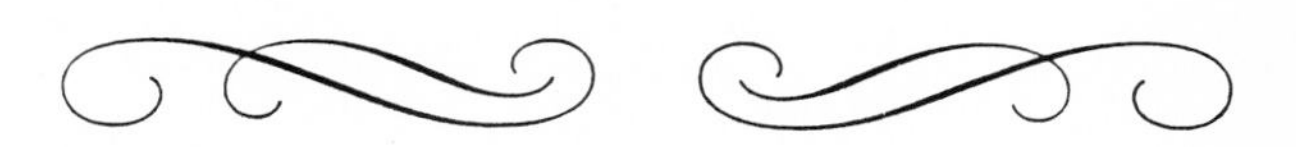

George MacBeth

JONATHAN CAPE
THIRTY-TWO BEDFORD SQUARE LONDON

First published 1986

Jonathan Cape Ltd, 32 Bedford Square, London WC1B 3EL

British Library Cataloguing in Publication Data

MacBeth, George
Dizzy's woman.
I. Title
823'.914[F] PR6063.A13

ISBN 0 224 02801 4

Typeset by Computape (Pickering) Ltd, North Yorkshire
Printed in Great Britain by
Ebenezer Baylis and Son Ltd
The Trinity Press, Worcester and London

Preface

THE EARL OF BEACONSFIELD – late Benjamin Disraeli – died in the spring of 1881, one of the most respected figures in England, a former Prime Minister, a popular novelist, and a mourning widower. But *der alte Jude* (as Bismarck called him), or the sphinx of Israel, as his solicitor Rose more aptly dubbed him, was a venerable gentleman with a Past.

Disraeli's pre-marital affair with the voluptuous Henrietta Sykes in the 1830s has been well-documented in J. R. Bernard's *The Young Disraeli.* But this was not an isolated fling. Disraeli's wife Mary Anne had her reasons for being coy in her approach to the altar. We know that she was jealous, for example, of Frances Anne Vane-Tempest, Lady Londonderry, one of the richest, most fashionable, and privately notorious women of her day. In the early years of her marriage Lady Londonderry had been suspected of an affair with Alexander I, the Tsar of Russia. Her flirtations were widespread, and their extension to the brilliantly Byronic, and exotically Latinate, young Disraeli, a witty salon dandy if ever there was one, is hardly surprising.

The post-marital letters in the published correspondence of Disraeli with Lady Londonderry (Macmillan, 1938) are friendly and respectful, but the handful of pre-marital ones are more sprightly; and there is a significant breach of contact between 1839, the year of Disraeli's marriage, and the renewal of the correspondence in 1845. This gap is bridged only by a freezing letter from Lady Londonderry to Disraeli in August 1839, postmarked Ayrshire, where she was attending another lover's (Lord Eglinton's) mediaeval tournament.

This notoriously archaising tilting session, from which Disraeli chose to absent himself by selecting it as his wedding day, ended up as a muddy scramble, ruined by rain. Disraeli betrayed a morbid interest in the details until the end of his life, corresponding with numerous participants, and including a description of the jousting in his novel *Endymion*, as late as 1880. Victorian and modern commentators (down to Ian Anstruther in his gripping survey *The Knight and the Umbrella*) have tended to stress the chaos, emphasising the squelching shambles when the skies opened and the event was rained off. But the expectations of debauchery were merely sordidly underlined by this outcome. For many who rode up to take part – from old Etonian knights to criminal cutpurses – there were dreams of unbridled sexual sport, from bedroom billiards to fornication among the fir-trees. This was as true for Charlie Lamb importing a nymphet from Bangor as for the crook Elephant Smith with his whore in a closed carriage.

The healthy tradition of lechery in tournaments dates back to the fourteenth century, when all the strumpets of Paris travelled over to a famous tilt at Crécy. It was probably normal for the bloody lance to be bared as frequently between the sheets as in the lists. Pop festivals, if not wrestling matches, offer a modern continuation of the same interest.

My object in *Dizzy's Woman* has been to enlarge upon the yawning gap in Disraeli's correspondence with Lady Londonderry, and to populate the void with an appropriate prurience. What more likely than that the young buck who had been out with Henrietta Sykes at Sir Henry Smythe's hunt (on 'an Arabian mare, which I nearly killed: a run of thirty miles and I stopped at nothing') would have tried to wheedle financial backing for a trip up north to carry his lady's colours in the Ayrshire ploughland? The Eglinton Tournament was in some ways the last gasp of a Regency salaciousness, gauzed over as the first clean breath of a Victorian purity. The churning up of the sward into ordure-like soil mimes the trenchancy of the national emotions at play. Piano legs would soon be in frilly knickers, huge families on the go, and whorehouses booming. Bishops were already girding their loins to convert prostitutes. The great cauldron of Victorian sexuality was starting to steam.

In the bowl of this cauldron I have seen Disraeli and Frances Anne Vane-Tempest (Vane for short) as two naked, wrestling cannibals, eating and due to be eaten, the dishes and the prey of their times, virulent and miserable. I have assumed broken promises, postulated intercourse, allowed the male ego its traditional uninterrupted whine.

We view the boiling hell of the 1840s through the jaundiced eyes of the recently married Disraeli, debt-ridden, scheming, and newly elected to Parliament, with his wife's money and his wife's connections to wrench along his career. The date is 1842 – three years after the Tournament expired in slime – and we find Disraeli still smarting and fascinated, repelled by his former mistress's betrayal, and yet eager to renew his liaison if he can, and punish her pride, in time, by his rejection.

The one-sided correspondence (the sick underbelly of the intimate style we know from the letters to Disraeli's sister Sarah; the masculine, philanderer's tone from the memoirs of Castiglione – and Disraeli, after all, was an Italian by ancestry) unreels from the dressing-room at Grosvenor Gate, where Disraeli is packing to go on holiday, and penning, as he packs, the first of his twenty-four needling letters to the woman he hates to love, and loves to hate.

THE WEATHER IS really more than I can stand. I am in my short sleeves, with neither cravat nor waistcoat, and I still feel boiled as a Normandy lobster. The bedroom is a chaos of clothes, jewellery, books, papers, more clothes, smelling-salts, blue books, baskets, canes, hats, oh, I don't know what we haven't hauled out of drawers and thrown down to consider taking.

Three months in Paris, even at our old haunt, the Hôtel de l'Europe, will seem like a terrible exile from all that civilisation – that is to say, London – has come to mean, unless we make sure to have with us whatever toys or distractions we expect to need.

Mary Anne is a bobbing whirlwind in stockings and stays, ever in and out from behind her silk screen, with a bevy, so it seems to me, of attendant maids and acolytes. Actually, none other, of course, than Nina Rook, who has been her faithful companion-at-arms for as long as either of us can remember.

I make do with my own two hands. The expense of a valet is not yet one I feel ready to undertake. You may guess, my dear, that the long shadow of former inconveniences – need I say any more – has not yet been dispelled.

Mary Anne has a few thousand a year, and, yes, she has

really been more than generous, but the house is by no means a cheap one to keep up, and my creditors, by the dozen, I fear, are still there ready in the wings.

Dear Vane. You have never had that particular worry. With four country houses, and a place on the Thames, and a large establishment in London, you were always well-adapted to meet any sudden claim on your private purse.

Enough of that. My news. Well, the session was a busy one, and I have done my poor best to make some mark in the House. Alas, it has all been corn, corn and more corn. Hume, Ewart and Cobden. Hume, Ewart and American corn. I feel that I have ears of the wretched stuff coming out of my skull.

But then you will know the main lines of our thoughts and wrangles from your husband. Charles has made his bed, I fear, and must lie upon it, so far as politics may go. For that other bed, hung with silks, and with fine tassels, and sheets of damask, and pillows deep with down, well, Vane, I had rather see him laid off it, and I there again in his place.

However. Our life at Grosvenor Gate. What of that, you may ask? Well, it's a comfortable house, and it does very well for access to the Commons, and a little occasional plotting, too, I may say. I had forty men to dinner in May, to show my face as a politician of new substance in the party.

But entertaining, other than that. Well, we do what we can. I never see Lady Jersey now, any more than I ever see Lady Londonderry, more's the pity. The *grandes-dames* of our touchy London society have not all been as pleased to see their Dizzy wedded as one might have hoped.

The Rothschilds have dropped in and out, of course. And the Montefiores. Jewish people. Jewish money. Mary Anne has become quite an expert at not speaking of Christian names.

She is ever tactless, yes. But she has her kind heart. And

she runs the house like a railway train. Everything, from breakfast to mulled wine before bedtime, is arranged on a plan. A very pleasant and helpful plan.

I confess that I like the change. I really do. Inside my wanderer's breast there beat a heart that sought for a settled home, and a doting bride. Well, I have them now. And I am well content.

Fairly well, anyway. There are still heights to scale in the political Switzerland, and some peaks that I have my eye on in the social Tyrol, as well. Time will provide the chance. Time, and an eye for opportunity.

Meanwhile, I remember old friends occasionally, and even meet one or two. I fell in with Maclise the other day in the Strand and walked with him as far as his new studio. He showed me a wonderful drawing of a knight thrusting a lance into a squirming dragon.

It had all that energy and maturity of line that he used to aim for, and often lacked. The Queen, he says, has given him some sort of commission, and I anticipate that we shall soon have a new Wilkie – an Irish one this time – to be adulating.

Painters are strange, though. He stood there in his floppy hat, with his head on one side, and the sheet of paper out at arm's length, and he seemed to be quite oblivious that I was there.

'Daniel,' say I, 'you are lost in the contemplation of your own genius. I shall tiptoe softly out, and leave you to enjoy her favours.'

'Dizzy,' says he, taking my arm with a laugh, and a blush, 'you're right at that. Yes, I was thinking how good it seemed. You know, I could never have done a thing like that unless I'd walked up to the Eyre Arms, and seen young Jerningham go over the head of his horse. Lord Eglinton was the educator of us all.'

'All,' say I, 'well, who are the others, Daniel?'

Then he took a turn around his room, straightening a

curtain here, and pulling a veil across an indiscreet nude there, and generally providing a picture of someone trapped in a potentially embarrassing situation.

'Who is it this time, Daniel?' I asked, with a touch of an edge to my voice, I have no doubt. 'One of the Sheridan girls? Or are the Irish immune to your Irish charm?'

'You never know, Dizzy,' he said, rising and leading me to a cabinet by the door. 'Now, let's have a glass of amontillado and talk of your own affairs. Lady Londonderry, for example. How is Vane?'

How indeed.

You never do reply to my letters. You're always off in Russia, or away in Yorkshire inspecting those coal-mines of yours they say are doing so well.

Coal, indeed! It might have been kohl, once, but never coal. I hardly expected to see my frivolous charmer become an industrial magnate in her own right. I heard from your son that you spend more time down on the coast at Seaham Hall than up in the woods at Wynyard now.

Dear Frederick. He makes me feel so old. There's only a year between us, of course, but I have the duties of a married man. Frederick is ever the young blood. I hear of him doing prodigious deeds amidst the brandy and water set at Bangor.

What a fellow to have for a son, Vane! If only a step. I confess I've wondered more than once, in my jealous days, if he'd ever been a lover as well as a son.

'Mother,' said Frederick to me, when I saw him the other day at Bright's, 'mother is quite the mistress of the mines nowadays. She speaks of you often, you know. And with real affection. You ought to write to her more. You really ought.'

Well, I took that with a pinch of snuff. I can tell you that. I bought him a glass of hock and admired his Moorish boots, and heard all about his encounters with the bandits in Egypt and how he'd been painted in a fez with an Arab houri by John Frederick Lewis.

Then he brought up the subject of the mines.

'She sleeps', he informed me, splendid as ever, I must confess, in his white necktie and plum tailcoat, 'in the very bed that Byron consummated his marriage in. Byron's bed, Dizzy, think of that. And outside, the great sands where he galloped his horse, reaching all the way to Sunderland.'

'A romantic spot,' I agreed.

'Romantic,' says Frederick, with a laugh, my dear, you could hear across the club. 'For you and me, Dizzy, it might well be Arabella and the Millbanke millions that would lift our hearts on those Yorkshire shores. But not mother's. No. She thought Byron vulgar, you know, and perhaps he was after the Tsar. Women are snobbish creatures. Mother is quite immune to the Byron charm. It's the black diamonds she smacks her chops over, the sweating Geordies down there under the clay.'

'Sweating,' I say.

'Sweating,' says Frederick. 'Boys of twelve, and, yes, Dizzy, women, too, stripped to the waist and labouring side by side in temperatures of a hundred degrees with only a quart of beer and a hunk of bread and cheese to keep them fit for the job. They say conditions on the Wiltshire farming estates are bad. They should see the miners cutting mother's coal.'

'Disgusting,' I say. 'We must sponsor a Bill, Frederick.'

'Disgusting, yes,' cries he. 'But think of the profit. Mother has a stone office there in the middle of the town with the family coat of arms up above the door and a pair of ledgers open on her desk, and the factors come in one after another, turning their hats in their greasy fingers, and she pays her miserable ten shillings a week and builds a hospital for their stunted wives to give birth to their rickety babies in, and says yes, Mr Scrimp, and no, Mr Scrounge, and rests her bum on her bags of gold like Mrs Midas in person.'

He despises you, Vane, you see, but he gives you a very attractive and business-like appearance. Bourgeois to the very bone. I can hardly believe a word of it. The blood of the Vane-Tempests can hardly have grown so muddy with charcoal dust.

So write, Vane. If I don't coax you, let me goad you into a fresh correspondence. I find it very enlivening, in the cool purlieus of my married life, to think of your grinding toil amidst the slither of shovel and the prod of pickaxe. Is it all the sweat of your brow, though, or is there also, I wonder, a little sweat of the belly, too?

Our worthy MacAlpine has just come in and told me the carriage is at the door. The bags must be clasped and strapped, and the baskets and trunks all taken down and stowed.

I shall finish with a flourish. This heat! I can almost feel the sweat fall on the page. Forgive me, Vane. May it bring you the scent of remembered spoils, the aroma of battle.

Tomorrow we sail. Tonight I shall sleep in Dover, with Mary Anne by my side. The packet will rock at the quay, and the waves lap the shore of the England I am leaving. How very Byronic it all sounds!

Reply if you will. I have, I may say, a special reason for hoping more than usual that you may put pen to paper at last. And of this, if I hear from you, I shall write in my next.

In the meantime, eat, sleep, and enjoy your family. And your colliers. I envy their jetty seams. George Smythe, by the way – you remember young George, old Strangford's boy – will be coming over to Paris on his way to Geneva. He has agreed to be my clandestine post office, and will carry news from my solicitor, and my agents. One needs a discreet emissary, in these reduced circumstances. I should hate Mary Anne to know all my business.

You may, therefore, share a packet with duns and Parliamentary place-seekers, with women who plot for my bed and with men who are after my money. You may lie, I say, between a bill and a *billet-doux*, my dear. What an opportunity! So, farewell.

AMAZING TO HAVE got your letter before we sailed! I had never supposed my communication would find you in London and with pen in hand, as it were, to consume your indignation in instant response. Stormy weather in Piccadilly, and stormy weather in Kent. I praise their conjunction.

Amazing, of course, to have got your letter at all. Well. I knew I could flush the coverts with a strike at your moral principles. Mixed in, as you say, with some grossly indecent innuendoes about your relations with your employees.

Let me take your points one by one. Of course it was a joke about sponsoring a Bill. My current position in the councils of the Tory party is somewhere between whore's hairdresser and butcher's boy. That is to say, I am needed but I am despised.

It will change, Vane. But be assured that your over-privileged mining-workers, as you so eloquently urge that they are, are not at the head of my list of the under-attended to. I have housing higher amongst my priorities than wages, and your men, you say, are all in stone cottages. Lucky fellows. To have such a priceless mistress.

And so you are, Vane. So you were. I see you still as you seemed that first night when Charles introduced us – at your own request, I remember – in your dress 'literally embroidered', I think I wrote to my sister Sarah, 'with emeralds and diamonds'.

You always liked that encrusted, rather Elizabethan look. The eyes of a tiger, and the skin of a jewelled rhinoceros. It was fortunate that the skin could be lifted – almost plate by plate, as it were – in the conservatory at Rosebank.

They could hear your squeals across the river at Kew. I had to gag you with your French knickers.

At any rate, I am sure you enjoy enough of that with your Yorkshire blackamoors. Or do you pine at times, I wonder, for my Jewish diligence?

Jewish diligence has been hard tried of late. What with Maclise. And then, of course, bumping into old Samuel Pratt, and, virtually, into young William Eglinton.

I was on my way to Brown's for a stimulating liquor and a dry chat with George Smythe. There was a sudden loud crumble of thunder, a particularly bright, almost blue, flash, and then there was a wall, a grey solid iron sheet, it seemed, of an icy, impenetrable, entirely unexpected, and deplorably biting rain.

I had barely time to turn my collar up, and wish my cane was a black umbrella, and run for shelter. But then, imagine my surprise, posing irresolutely on the corner of Bond and Maddox Street, to find myself sharing the rain, as it were, with a solitary, and for the moment stationary, companion.

Unlike myself, he seemed unbothered by the thunderstorm. Gleaming, as it seemed, from some internal source of light, as if he had a private stock of sunshine locked up under his breastplate, this golden man-at-arms – or no, I now realised, with a glance through his open visor at the empty interior, this golden man of arms, for such he was, a mere gilded iron suit of armour – was prepared evidently to stand out the rain as he was, unprotected and undismayed.

Then, 'Quickly, lad, or the suit will rust away,' I heard a familiar unctuous voice declare, and, lo and behold, a yard away on the streaming pavement there materialised, first, a gangling sixteen-year-old in a tight green velvet waistcoat and a pair of buckskin breeches, and then, close behind, under the most enormous umbrella I have ever seen, an umbrella to end all umbrellas, an *umbrellissima*, Vane, the short, stocky figure, dark as an undertaker in his brushed shagreen and lizardskin, of the proprietor of this suit of armour, Samuel Pratt, Esquire.

'Quickly, quickly, boy,' he was entreating, grappling as he spoke with bolt and rivet in a hopeless attempt to unshackle his man of gold and iron and convey him piecemeal, as it were, indoors. The rain, meanwhile, being no respecter of persons or knights of armour, continued to batter down in a solid soaking wall, drowning out screams of deluged ladies, yells of irate, watered-down swells, and indeed, I suspect, my own gulps of outraged dripping.

'Pratt,' I shouted, however, above the tumult, 'allow me, old fellow, to give you a hand with that ancient metal monstrosity.'

So, pausing only for one startled, thankful glance, and a regretful laying aside of his immense but encumbering umbrella, Pratt laid hands on one of the armoured legs, gestured to me to grasp the other, and nodded to his boy to clutch at the torso. And thus, between the saturated three of us, the golden armour of Archibald William, 13th Lord of Eglinton – for indeed, Vane, it was Eglinton's own long-bartered and battered suit – was clanked and hauled, groaning and squelching, into the comparative safety of the doorway from which Pratt had emerged.

'Well, now,' I said, shaking water off the brim of my hat. 'It really is the sporting Earl's very own glad metal rags.'

'Mr Disraeli,' said the snake-like Pratt, all grease and slither again, it seemed, in the narrow corridor, 'you are ever present at the vital moment. I thank you, sir, and with all my heart. Now, I don't suppose', he added with a scaly rub of his fingers, 'that you would be interested in making a purchase of this excellent memento of that melàncholy occasion. Thus aptly christened, if one may use the term, with a suitable blemish of holy water?'

'No, Pratt,' I demurred, 'your prices, I do suspect, are well beyond the means of a poor near Israelite such as me.'

'Then sherry, sir,' he insisted, and sherry we drank, from a brace of thin-lipped and exquisite Spanish glasses that once graced, he assured me, the table of the Empress Isabella.

Well, there was talk, Vane, much talk of that flagrant extravagance, that wastrel and yet so chivalrous bonanza, the brain-child of the Earl of Eglinton, his marvellous and so catastrophic Tournament.

'There is there a tale to be told,' said Pratt, sipping his oloroso. 'A theme worthy the pen of a great master, Mr Disraeli.'

'Tennyson,' I suggested, for, after all, one was hearing so much of his new volume, 'Alfred Tennyson might well be prevailed upon to give it the delicate Arthurian touch.'

'Scarcely that,' said Pratt, with a dry, python-chuckle. 'This was a modern matter, a money affair. No scope for the high-falutin niceties of a blank verse epic. I would rather read Thackeray, or even Dickens, on the story of the Eglinton Tournament.'

I took my leave rather soon after that, Vane, you may be sure. Thackeray, indeed! A spluttering fool with a pen dipped in vinegar. And Dickens. Well, you know my views about him.

'The rain has left the street well-rinsed,' said Pratt, as he saw me off at the door, nodding his long head this way and that as if about to strike some passer-by in the neck and suck his blood out, 'as that other rain left the fields of

Ayrshire. Yes, Mr Disraeli. Someone should certainly try his hand at a novel about the Tournament.'

Then he put his fingers cold on my wrist, and paused for a swift second looking up into my eyes.

I SAW GEORGE SMYTHE this morning, strolling in the Tuileries, and he gave me your letter. What fun this cape and dagger stuff can be! But fraught, alas, with many a practical difficulty.

Using George as a post-box ought to work rather well so long as he's in Paris, but he plans to travel in Switzerland, and then in Italy. I suppose I shall have to give the commission to Baillie-Cochrane.

Not, Vane, a very enticing prospect. Young George is leading a life as disreputable as one might wish, and he sees the point of being a sort of unofficial receiver. The other – oh, dear – is, I fear, much too puritanical.

Still, they are both of my party now. With Manners we make a band of four, pledged, I may say, to stand like a fortress next session in support of what we believe. And Baillie-Cochrane is anxious to keep his place.

I shall simply have to tell him the correspondence is all political. And highly secret. As indeed a certain proportion of it is. Poor Mary Anne! She was nearly out of her mind when she came upon a dunning letter from Austen one day at Grosvenor Gate. If she ever discovers the full extent of my debts I shall never hear the end of it, Vane.

As for such letters as this – dear and sweetly passionate

letter from my love – her jealousy would know no bounds if she were even to suspect that such a thing might exist. She threw a vase at me once during our courtship.

Excuse me. I shall close the window. We have a very pleasant suite of rooms here overlooking the Gardens, but the noise of the children playing can be a distraction. I am on my own, Vane, unshaven as yet and in my shirt-sleeves, and enjoying a glass of hock and soda-water in lieu of breakfast.

I don't know what it is, but Paris seems to bring out the Byron in me. At any rate, I have pen and paper, and a fascinating piece of news to tell. Eglinton is in Paris!

He has been staying in Provence, and hunting boar with the Duc d'Orléans, and will be present, so Manners assures me, at the salon of the Duchesse de Grammont on Friday.

The noise is really too enervating. I shall confine myself, Vane, to a brief letter and a rather more extensive post-scriptum, to be composed on Saturday morning after my Eglinton encounter. I wonder if I shall have been able to bring your name into the conversation? Let us wait and see.

What a change there is in Eglinton! It must be that very imprudent marriage of his. For a 13th Earl to marry the widow of a naval officer, and, after all, one, as a natural child, with no legal existence – well, Vane, that was surely a somewhat amazing, if not dashing and obstinate, action.

I gather that she has made him give up his hunting, too, and he talks, forsooth, of selling the stud. Lord Eglinton! To dispose of his precious horses, and leave the turf! I could hardly believe my ears.

Eglinton, I may say, has acquired a slight stoop – one can almost feel the onset of middle age already – but he still carries himself with the same rather dour Scottish boniness. Like a skeleton entangled with a rawhide whip.

I arranged to meet him again for a private breakfast on Sunday, and Sunday coming, which was yesterday, to give you the full and precise detail of my timing, we drank our tea and ate a roll together at a small open-air café in the Champs de Mars, and I was made for the first time privy to the original inspiration, if I may so call it, which led to the eventual full and deliberate flowering of the Eglinton Tournament.

It makes a bizarre tale. Imagine, if you will, that square-shaped wedding-cake of a castle up in the rainy wilds of Ayrshire. Not, as you knew it so well, on the momentous occasion in 1839 when I was so busy tying the knot of marriage. Not then, Vane. But a mere ten, dragging, inelegant years before, when the future hero of the lists, and Lord of the Tournament, is a gangling lad of fifteen, gaunt in Hamlet face and ruffled sleeves, and with buckskin trousers soiled from chasing rabbits, and a billiard cue in his hand.

Outside, of course, the rain is pouring down, as usual, on the shaggy Highland cattle, and the muddy ha-ha, and the bedraggled parterres, and the wooded purlieus and the flowery policies. The lake, indeed, is positively spitting with rain.

So Eglinton said. Spitting with rain. He'd been out with a rod and line to trail for perch but he'd been driven in by the weather. So there he was, wringing out his shirt-sleeves on his own best Aubusson carpet on the floor of the billiard-room, and lamenting the absence of anything interesting to do, while his stepfather sat upstairs in the green saloon swilling burgundy and playing nap with a brace of randy gamekeepers, and his plain mother lay prone in her boudoir, snoring away the after-effects of too much pheasant pie for luncheon.

I add one or two details of my own, of course. Lady Montgomerie always struck me as far too heavy an eater for someone anxious to be the seductress she thought she was. And as for Sir Charles Lamb, that hook-nosed old corsair was the nearest thing to the god Pan in tailcoat and hunting-boots I ever met.

Anyway, there stood Eglinton, bored and wet. And there beside him, immaculate in a black velvet suit of jacket and knickerbockers – like a sort of Satanic copy of Gainsborough's Blue Boy, I suppose – crossing his legs and nursing one of his guinea-pigs, lounged Charlie Lamb.

This was the year, I gather, when Charlie had just turned twelve and Eglinton himself was nearly sixteen. They were both at Eton still, but that was a connection very shortly, as we shall see, to be severed.

Charlie was very dusky, according to Eglinton, and was nicknamed 'the black beauty' at school, although, to be sure, I doubt very much if his colour went any closer to a light varnish than my own does.

He was quite the dandy, too, it seems. Elderly-seeming in his precocious way, with a style of affecting the Beau Brummells a bit. As if it was still 1795, and he was in Bath, and master of ceremonies. A formidable and rather frightening squib of a fellow for twelve years old, I imagine.

'William,' he says, with a carefully affected sort of sprawl, scarcely a drawl, in his voice. 'You are vewy wet. Sir Masterful Pwescience is not amused at Your Wetness.'

He had a habit, says Eglinton, of constantly varying the names of his guinea-pigs, of which he had several dozen, and thus presenting them, according to his mood, in any one of a hundred alternative, but invariably noble and grandiose, titles.

'Charlie,' says Eglinton, and I guess the fervour in his voice down the years, 'I am bored. What shall we do?'

Charlie rises, brushing imaginary flecks of dust from his waistcoat, while he carefully rests his knightly familiar in the crook of his arm. He gazes out through the immense mullioned and transomed affair that some Ayrshire Pugin has foisted off on Eglinton's grandfather as Gothic.

'Tewwibly hard to say, William,' he replies. 'I imagine the only thing is to ask Sir Distinguished Arbiter to interpwet the mood of the day.'

He was very Bunyanesque at that date, you see.

So William bends over the billiard-table, and knocks the three balls about for a while, while Charlie consults the guinea-pig about what to do.

'Lord Affluence and Integwity is very doubtful,' says Charlie, shaking his head. 'The wain distwacts the indications.'

'Tell you what,' says William, pocketing a ball. 'Would Lord Affluence care to step out of allegory and back into heraldry for the day? I could hardly bear another plod through the Slough of Despond, Charlie.'

Upstairs, meanwhile, the house is waking up. Lady Montgomerie is shaking sleep from her ears, and picking up her stitching, and beginning to reflect on the possibilities of an affair with the Duke of Buccleuch. Sir Charles is losing tenner after tenner and deciding to switch from nap to piquet, and for lower stakes, and perhaps with that rather lovely second chambermaid instead of these ill-bred and far too skilful yokels.

'I know,' cries Charlie suddenly, with a clap of his hands, and a click of his teeth. 'Sir Flodden Field has made up his mind. The auguwies are auspicious. We must hold a tournament.'

'A tournament,' says Eglinton, scratching his head. 'I'm not sure about that, Charlie. Using the spears, you mean?'

In the lofty octagonal hall the lances creak in their leather girths, the shields glisten and echo to the remote boom of a gong, the winter flies gather on the helmet of Eglinton's ancestor, who slaughtered the King of France with a misjudged jab of his wooden rod in 1539.

Charlie, however, has something more miniature in mind. He walks to the table. He reaches over and strokes the green baize with his pudgy hand.

'Sir Flodden,' he calls over his shoulder. 'Awise and make thy challenge to all comers. Twead the field in all your glorwy.'

And before the astonished Eglinton knows what the boy is about, Charlie has lifted the scruffy white guinea-pig and set it down, feet splayed out, nose alert, ears on the turn this way and that for trouble, on the very centre line of the table.

After that, I gather, and Eglinton was very good on the details, the whole thing developed into a full-scale catastrophe. He became quite keen at first, he remembers, and helped lug down the special military chest, a massive affair that might have served the Duke of Wellington in person, with brass handles, and inlay in satinwood – the chest, apparently, in which the more especially favoured of Charlie's brood of beknighted rodents made their travels. On beds of lettuce, it seems, and with little built-in bowls to drink their milk and water from.

So out they came, the black and the red and the russet, one after another, and up they went, foot after foot after curly tail, nervous or diffident, outraged or somnolent, incontinent or in perfect cleanliness, into their palanquins in the half dozen pockets. From there, whiskers questing, they surveyed the field of honour.

Meanwhile, alas, the house continued to stir. The rain continued flooding down on horn of Highland bull and on gill of unguddled trout, the hands of the great ormolu clocks turned slowly round in their gilded frames, and the thoughts of servants and family were turned in their mental frames towards the notion of tea.

'A gage, a gage, I do declare,' cries Charlie suddenly, bending over the table with sleeves rolled up now to marshal his champions, and indeed, poor Eglinton recalled, there *was* a very clear-cut evidence of a certain something thrown down on the sward. It stood, he says, and it smelled.

The guinea-pigs milled this way and that, in pocket or on cushion, shouldering each other rather more in the manner of boys at an Eton wall-game than proper knights of the fifteenth century in the elegant stress of battle. But shouldering, yes, and giving evidence of a fine mêlée.

We sat there at our small marble table in the sun, Vane, and he smiled that slow Scottish smile of his, and I watched him recall the whole merry scene from all those years back.

'What happened next?' I asked.

'Well, you know, Dizzy,' he told me, 'the fur of the guinea-pigs, and the mess on the baize, and the whole sense of a sort of rough and tumble in a special place, it somehow caught my imagination. I didn't know it had at the time, but it had. What with Charlie and his fancy talk, when the Queen decided to forgo her coronation, or at least the more splendid aspects of it, I decided that I would repeat that scene of the guinea-pigs on the billiard-table, but with real people, and a real jousting-ground, and without, this time, any interruption from the outside world.

'You see, Dizzy,' he went on, 'it was all a bit of a cataclysm up in Scotland that afternoon. We were in the thick of the thing, with Charlie and me cheering on our favourites, and the guinea-pigs growing really rather involved, and getting into the spirit of the business, and starting to scamper about, and push each other in quite a belligerent fashion, I thought, when suddenly, in comes my darling mother, all of a tizzy and asking why we haven't heard the bell for tea and behind her there is my stepfather, face like a worn-out hatchet handle, and, Lord, then he sees the state of the billiard-table, and, well, after all it was my own billiard-table like everything else in the house when all was said and done, but the roof still seemed to come off the house and he swore like a sub-lieutenant at Talavera with a poison spider down his breeches.

'To cap it all, Dizzy, Charlie and I were taken out of Eton, which was thought to have been a bad influence, and to have put ideas into our heads, and for the rest of our adolescence we stayed at home, and had a private tutor, and improved, I may say, our game of billiards, on the freshly covered table, beyond recognition.

So there it is. Charlie Lamb and his guinea-pigs were really the beginning of the whole business.'

Then he commiserated with me because I never finally rode in the Tournament, and that brought, I'm afraid, the hint of a manly tear to my eye, Vane, and I took my leave soon after, and left him to pay the bill, and came back here, and had to postpone the writing of this rather lengthy, but still, I hope, not too entirely tedious, postscriptum until this morning. But more of that in time.

PEEL IS ADAMANT. I had a letter this morning. Not a morsel of power shall I taste. Not one. So I fancy that the choice is between the higher journalism, if I may so describe my scribbling for *The Times*, or the lower sorts of fiction.

You may well suppose that the savaging I got for *Venetia* would have turned me against the notion of writing a silver fork affair for ever. Well, it has.

No more society satires for me. The time has come for a new sort of tale. Something to out-Carlyle Carlyle at his own radical game. A Tory novel with a conscience.

I am scribbling away today in the gardens. We seem to be having a last splash of October sun before the cold douche of the French winter, and the dogs are all out having their day. I never saw so many Pomeranians in pink ribbons.

And all their mistresses with parasols and straw bonnets as if it was still the middle of June. The Parisians are more optimistic than we English about the weather.

Last night, by the way, I was introduced to the King. Am I casual enough about such a thing? I hope I am, Vane. When the blood of Aramaic emperors, who ruled before Judah was Judah, or Tyre Tyre, may be said to flow through my tautly Semitic veins, who am I, you may think, to be much impressed by the court of a summary Bourbon?

Who, indeed? But the conversation, though brief and not very political, was a great success. We got on, Vane. We got on very well. I shall see him again, I know, though the court is not, as it were, in session, and thus Mary Anne, alas, may not be presented to the Queen.

We spoke of the season mostly, and the state of English letters, on which, as you may believe, I had much to say, but I have my hopes of a more intriguing and closely social chat at a later date.

Are you in Ireland still? I think your idea to put up a Gothic castle upon your estate is a splendid notion. Has Charles any objection? I always think of him as a very Georgian fellow still, at least so far as the architectural arts are concerned.

Not so, of course, his near namesake, sweet young Charlie Lamb. I had meant to go on a whit about him and his guinea-pigs in my last letter, until the thought of my not being there at the Tournament, and you being fêted and wined as the Queen of the Castle, quite overcame my inclination.

William Eglinton was very droll about the guinea-pigs, and a little tender and poignant, too, I must confess. They were very close once, he and Charlie, and I think the family feeling is still a strong one.

Charlie, it seems, was born and brought up for many years at Beauport, in Sussex, a mile or two, as I gather, from where the Battle of Hastings is said to have been fought out. So the early influence of King Harold and the Norman Conquest was a powerful one on the burgeoning fantasies of the boy.

He knew whatever there was to know about knights in armour, and fine ladies held in towers, and the right way to draw a bow, and the wrong way to express an achievement, or quarter a shield, before he was even seven years old. He had little books he drew up, so Eglinton says, with a full heraldic history of the Lambs and their allies, with coloured arms and mottoes in Latin going right back to the twelfth century.

The Lambs, however, were only a secondary interest. Their pedigree, though long, was limited by the facts of history. Not so the family trees for the guinea-pigs, who began, so Eglinton said, to become a consuming passion for Charlie by the time he was ten.

He found one dying, I believe, on a cold winter's day in a stubble-field, and took it home, and sat with it in his hands until its eyes finally closed, and he vowed then, and wrote his vow down in gold paint on a strip of vellum, too, that he would thenceforward honour the heirs and ancestors of the guinea-pig line, chosen as he had been by death to be their scribe.

It's come on very chill. I think I shall take my writing-case and my pen indoors and continue over a cup of chocolate at Le Cygne.

That's better. The warming draught has brought a new flood of ease to my fancy.

Yes, a strange fellow, Charlie. He began, in 1827, and continued for nearly ten years, a complete account of the life and times of the seventeen guinea-pigs which became, very shortly, and in return for a small expenditure on the part of his indulgent papa, the establishment of Castle Falling.

He took the name, I think, from hearing of Castle Rising, and then deciding that his was already finished, and was even, so his melancholy spirit insisted, in the days of its gradual decline. So Castle Falling took on an ivy-clad, and moth-surrounded, and somewhat doom-laden atmosphere, even before the final wooden planks, carefully planed and prepared by the estate carpenter, had been knocked and nailed and dovetailed into place.

'It was, of course, Dizzy,' so Eglinton remembered, as we stretched our boots in the sun, 'a very Gothic affair, with crockets and pinnacles and a mass of octagonal towers with flagstaffs and pennants flying. It was all done very well. Old Bonedragon, our estate carpenter, had slapped the whole box together with a lot of skill, and a mite of love.

'It was a hutch to end all hutches. A real fortress with a moat dug in the flower-beds, and with elders growing round it, and a little walled garden, and a stable block, rather bigger than the Castle actually, where the two King Charles's spaniels who drew the guinea-pigs' carriages were installed.

'I used to play with the guinea-pigs myself, but Charlie, I must admit, was happier with them on his own. They were much too real to be shared with someone who saw them merely as pets, and that's what they were, when all was said and done, to me.

'There were four rather special ones, the eldest of which, a huge obese black male, of indeterminate age, was known as the Duke of Bumbleby, or sometimes, in deference to an obscure Neapolitan title, according to Charlie, as Lord Ratatouille. He was very much the King of the Castle, anyway, and used to lounge his days away in a regal suite of rooms on the upper floor, immediately below the battlements.

'He had a sort of Queen, or skinny mistress, of a rusty-brown colour, with magnificent long silky white whiskers, and she was always referred to as Lady Single-blood, except at Christmas and Easter, when she sported another title, Lady Mary of the Angels.

'Charlie, you know, had a strong Catholic streak in his make-up, although he was officially, by the time he was nine, a convinced atheist, and would shock his poor old rakehell Regency father by calmly announcing at dinner that the Holy Spirit was all a sham, and the divinity of Jesus Christ a very open question, and up to each man to decide for himself.

'Of course, he had his bottom tanned for this, and was

instructed never to say or think such things again, and to read his brass-bound Bible for half an hour every night and morning, but Charlie simply opened the book at random, and kept his mouth shut, and learned a great deal of obscure genealogy from Deuteronomy and Leviticus, and got a reputation, clever lad, for being obedient and recanting his opinions.

'I think he did revere the externals of Christianity, though, as he does nowadays, you know, with his visits to Ely and Salisbury, and all his talk about the civilising influence of Pugin, and the fun of Kenelm Digby, and the need to accept the ritual and the ceremony and forget about all the stupid faith and good works.

'A rum customer, our Charlie, Dizzy. So he called his third main guinea-pig – or usually did, you see he could never bear to do without a good new name he'd thought up, and he was always adding further titles to his creations, very much, I suppose, as the Crown and the House of Lords are prone to do – he called his third one, I say, Lord Peter Ploughwright of Plumblossom.

'Lord Peter was a pure albino, white skin, red eyes, white ropy tail and all. A swan of a lord and guinea-pig-at-arms, if ever I saw one. I liked him best of all. He had a sort of mournful, wistful look in his red eye, as if he'd had rather too much iced claret and fancied another glass.

'His mate or friend, or supporter, or comrade-at-arms, or what you will, was a very big, broad, burly guinea-pig, with a flat head and a patch of mange in his dun fur. Not very prepossessing, but strong and full of character. Wilful and a bit surly.

'He became known as the Marquess of Mild Manners, partly ironically, I think, because of his temperament and also, I suppose, in deference to that spirit of respect for Bunyan that never seemed to leave Charlie.

'The others, fourteen at first, as I say, and then rather more, and then less, as they bred or died, or wandered away on missions or pilgrimages and were found choked in their moat, or strangled by an alley-cat, or bitten through the neck by a mastiff, well, they were all the heirs, descendants, dependants, retainers and what have you of the main four.

'They all had their own rooms, well-furnished with straw and seeds and water, and with coats of arms on the doors, carefully tinted and altered from time to time by Charlie in person, who could lean over the battlements and reach down into corridor or over architrave with his brush and paint-box.

'It was really very much a labour of love for Charlie. He would spend hours there, alone or with me or one of the servants in tow, sleeves rolled up, or little velvet cape flung aside, working away in snow or in sunshine to keep his world of guinea-pigs well-oiled, as it were, and in running order.

'It was very much a machine; indeed, a sort of mechanical re-creation of the Middle Ages, like the sort of entertainment you could see any day at Asprey's Theatre for a shilling and sixpence, but done here with real passion, and real care, and real understanding.

'Charlie knew what he was doing. He'd read almost every book there ever was about chivalry, and he had the imagination to twist the details around a bit, and give them a new life of their own. He'd read his Walter Scott, of course, met the old boy once at Abbotsford, indeed, and he was able to be more of the poet than the pedant about his castle.

'The biggest moment, and the saddest, too, I suppose, was when there was a great storm one night – and, yes, Dizzy, I can see it might seem like a premonition – and the rain burst through the leads of Castle Falling, and flooded through the upper floors, and the poor old Duke of Bumbleby was trapped in his room and drowned amidst his beds of straw with his narrow Queen there in his arms.

'There had, of course, to be an enormous double funeral. The royal house, as it were, had been wiped out at a single stroke. Well, it hadn't, I know. It had many heirs, I'm sure, to carry it on. But the line of succession was insecure, and Charlie was determined to look on the black side of things.

'He had his mother send out for a jet silk shawl, and a new toy carriage specially painted all in black and gold, and the bodies of the Duke and Lady Mary of the Angels were draped in scented voile and gauze, and then laid side by side on what Charlie was pleased to call their gun carriage, and there were blasts on a toy trumpet, and the steady beating of a drum, and the funeral cortège, drawn by the brace of spaniels at a carefully slowed pace, went three times round the front lawn, and then back to the burial plot in the shrubbery of azaleas behind the herb garden.

'There Charlie officiated at the burial service, dressed in black from head to foot, black shirt, black silk hat, black gloves and shoes, and his now, alas, very battered and ancient, but still black velvet, Gainsborough suit.

'The other mourners were Bonedragon, the under-gardener, a pimply boy of nineteen, and myself. No one else was invited, and no one else came. What with the rain streaming down, and the wind howling in the bare bushes, it's not surprising that no one very much minded missing their invitation.

'"Ashes to ashes," Charlie murmured, waving a sort of ebony wand like a small magician. "Fur to fur. She loved him and he loved her. This is a very twagic occasion. I say no more."

'However, there had to be some kind of reading, so Charlie thought, though not, in conformity with his beliefs, from the Bible. Instead, we were treated, sopping and cold as we were, to a fifteen-minute mumbled intonation from *The Manual of Chivalry*, and then a short recitation from *The Song of Roland*, in Old French.

'It was all really very weird, and also very touching, in about equal proportions, Dizzy, like everything else about young Charlie Lamb. And it made a lasting impression.'

So there you are. The full story of Charlie Lamb and the folly of the guinea-pigs. I must draw towards a conclusion or I shall miss my chance to get this into the evening bag.

You hint in your own postscriptum that there may be a chance of your coming over with Charles to Fontainebleau in November. Well now, I wonder. Were it not for my debts, I might rent a room in the Bois, or near to it, and have commerce there with my heart's desire, like a common whore.

Come, Vane, you enjoy these naughty thoughts, I know you of old. I can feel your lips moistening at the very idea of being treated as Harriette Wilson was by the Earl of Craven. Be honest now.

So tell me your plans. I feel very lustful towards you, and very tender. You know I do. I really must end now and have this in the hands of Smythe for a rush to the boat. I am anxious to hear your reply to my proposition.

Be swift, my love. Be lewd. And be generous. We could easily take the lease on a suite of rooms by the river on what you make in a single day, I hear, from those sweltering mines of yours in the north.

I AM FURIOUS THAT your plans to come over to Paris have, as you claim, to be cancelled. Of course I understand about Charles and the duties of being the new Lord Lieutenant of Durham. Indeed, I could scarcely be more delighted at the appointment.

We shall have some Tory magistrates at last. As you say, the Whig hegemony in Northumbria has come to a pretty pass when a publican has to have voted for Lord John Russell in order to get a licence.

But, Vane, surely these onerous liabilities under which our mutually respected Charles must labour are exactly the sort of thing he had best make sense of on his own. I should have thought a few weeks in society here amongst the de Beaufremonts and the de Marmiers would be just what you need to restore your complexion, and even your figure, for a winter return to the tasks of the Lord Lieutenant's wife.

I need your body. Those productive mines of yours, I fear, are too fascinating a distraction. They say in *The Times* that you held a banquet – which you yourself entirely fail to mention – for a guest list of – is this really true? – four thousand sweating colliers and their grubby wives.

You are working hard, my dear, to ward off the opprobrium of being classified as a vicious and cruel magnate. It will not be enough. You mark my words, the day will come when a law will be passed to prevent the employment of women and children under the ground.

Laugh if you will. The wheels grind very slow. But they grind, my dear. I am no admirer of Cobden or Bright, as well you know, but the future of England, Vane, is not to be sought in the steady increase of coal production, and the devastation of beautiful seascape in the interests of pioneering for new shafts.

You have shafts already for the pioneering. A fine twin pair, my darling. So abandon your new probing and give yourself over for the autumn to your old inspector of mines, your former overseer and steady worker at the kohl-face, B. Disraeli, Esq.

I shall await your change of mind. After all, you will hardly want to be up there holding his coat if Charles takes it into his head to be challenging some local butcher to a duel with pistols.

Vane. Am I growing a little pompous? I have paused to read over my last few sentences and I do detect, I fear, some hint of the hustings. I grow too political in my Froggish exile here.

Perhaps next year some office, even a small insignificant office, a minor position in the Board of Trade, will siphon away, as it were, this malaise of idle ranting. In the meanwhile, I shall watch my words.

I shall write with care. I have no desire to be written off as a mere poseur in the manner, Vane, of that idiot Monckton Milnes. Whom we cherish, of course, for his rich papa, and his place in Warwickshire, and his noble collection of indecent manuscripts.

But not, alas, for his poesy. Nor for his speeches, nor his talk at parties, and lisping at blues. Is it really so, by the by, that Stuart de Rothesay's girl has made her match with Waterford? I never believed he would get her as far as the gate, far less persuade her to lift her legs and jump.

I had always heard it said that she was the most exquisitely sweet and pure girl – amongst the unmarried maids, that is – at the Tournament. She must have been twenty-one that year. Is it possible that she can have failed to lose her virginity in those icy kyles of Bute?

I used to see Stuart de Rothesay in London at Molly Blessington's. We never realised that he was keeping such a pearly jewel shut away amidst his mists and his paddle-steamers.

He was back from Paris when I first met him, so I suppose the young lady must have cut her teeth on the language of Bluebeard and de Sade. A certain amount of backstairs embassy jargon, and keeping her youthful eyes open behind the canapés and the twirling fans, may have allowed some tiny hint of corruption, after all.

You don't give her much of a character, I must say. But I like your picture of her fawning round her chosen Henry's palanquin. You make her sound like a Dutch spaniel, on heat.

Am I to detect the rivalry of one coal baroness towards another, if I may assume that you see a future of competition from those Welsh mines of the Butes? Or is it a matter more, my dear, of the mutton seeing fit to throw mud on the lamb?

For me, you need have no fear. I had rather caress those mature haunches of yours than the rare thighs of a dozen underfed Lady Louisas. Let Waterford have her and welcome. I fancy, though, she'll see no more of the Marquess than the muddy soles of his riding-boots. It will still be the bay geldings of Killarney he puts his spurs into.

I shared a hansom with Alford yesterday on our way to dinner.

'Dizzy,' he said to me. Very confidingly, Vane, I may say, in a steamy whisper into my ear, with the soft sound of the rain starting to hiss outside on the canvas roof. 'I could tell you tales about Waterford that would sear your vitals.

'We were both in the same year – same house – at Eton. We were both beaten by Keate on the same day. Not, I should add, the famous day, when he laid the rod on the bottoms of seventy-nine boys in a single afternoon.

'Legend has had its say about that, of course. You will know the facts. Let me tell you, though, that the real reason was other than what they say. There was lack of discipline, oh yes. There was ever that.

'But it wasn't exactly a riot that the vicious old dominie was out to suppress. That, too, perhaps. But also the spread of a certain habit amongst the older boys. Do I make my meaning clear?

'Pilling was the word then popular at school. But I always prefer the more old-fashioned expression, tossing-off. There were seven boys discovered, I know, on the famous day – all interlinked like a series of Indian elephants carved in ivory. Trunk into trunk, as it were.

'I remember the lines forming, six by six, and the whole school paraded in hall to see justice done. Damned if I do remember the old boy's words in his speech about the business. Doubt if I took it in, anyway. I was only nine at the time.

'When Waterford and I got a slamming it was for shooting partridges. The same day and the same place as William Eglinton. But he bagged more than we did.'

Then I asked him about Waterford and his marriage. We were outside the Trianon by then, and I was down in the rain paying off the driver.

'Dizzy,' he said, 'I wish dear Waterford very well. I really do. But I hardly fancy he could get his broomstick up a floosie.

'In confidence, old fellow,' he added, with the sort of volume that ought to have made his confidence known to the whole of the nineteenth *arrondissement*, 'I should say that the Marquess of Waterford is a man for horses. Yes. And after that, a man for men.

'He can be a bugger for a bit of fun, of course. One summer he took a hunting-lodge in Connemara and spent a weekend shooting out the eyes of the family portraits with a pistol. He put a donkey into a stranger's bed at an inn. I could tell you a hundred tales about his mad ways.

'But I couldn't tell you a single piece of gossip where dear old Waterford has been having it away with a piece of French crackling. Unlike you or me, Disraeli, eh? Unlike you or me.'

I can tell you, Vane, I was very anxious to get the man off on his way by then.

Imagine me, Vane, immaculate in my cloak and silk hat, very English, too, I like to think, and with Mary Anne likely to emerge at any moment to find out why I was chatting away in the rain.

'Good night, Alford,' I said as firmly as I could, and then I was off up the steps, with a wave of my cane, and his voice trailing after me through the night.

'Not any more, though, Dizzy. Not any more. You with your Mary Anne, and I with my maid Marian. We're a couple of reformed characters, I fancy. A pair of poachers who've turned into the best gamekeepers in the business. Good night, old fellow. And good hunting. Tally ho, eh?'

Of course, he hated Waterford. I remember your telling me how he nearly killed him that second afternoon in the mêlée. Charles had to intervene as King of the Tournament and drag them apart.

So I took what he said with a pinch of snuff. I imagine the rivalry went back to their days at school.

They were always fighting and feuding. Shooting and riding. Pigeons or people. Horses or women.

So tell me, Vane. Tell me about your own childhood. What was it like to be a young lady in the early days of the nineteenth century? What was it like to be going to be very rich, and to marry a Duke?

Well, I know you didn't, or not exactly. But then Charles did turn out to be a Marquess, even if it took his brother's suicide to bring on the title. A mad bastard, was Castlereagh. That's what Lyndhurst used to say, with a lot of admiration in his voice. And, coming from Lyndhurst, the compliment was a sound one.

Well, they were all mad bastards, weren't they, Vane? Eglinton racing on foot for a wager to beat a man on a horse around a post and back. Castlereagh prosecuted, they say, for assaulting a boy dressed in women's clothes in a brothel. Charles, I have heard, seducing the mistress of Metternich, and pinching the bottoms of strange beauties on the stairs at the opera in Vienna. Were they male or female? Which, Vane?

What happened when the cabman nearly flogged him to death that night on the bridge? Was it just a quarrel over the fare? Or was there something else? I'll bet Metternich and his spies have a fine story in their log-books. A British ambassador, the golden peacock, as he was known, with his uniform all bloody about the crutch and the seat ripped open with a bayonet.

Well, well. So one has heard. A mad bastard. Why did you marry him, Vane? What did you want? Was it only marriage? It wasn't money, for sure. You had more than enough of that. Was it leisure? Was it, Vane? Was it space and energy to spare for your own amusements?

What did you learn on your father's country estates amongst the stable boys? Was it Jack Vane, your natural brother, who taught you your tricks? Jack Vane, who would never inherit the farms and the mine. Perhaps he made sure he'd inherit the body that was made to have it all.

Inherit or have. I feel very lustful again, Vane. Forgive my speculations. You must come and tell me the truth. With a tender honesty. With a slow, and reverent, love.

Which brings me to my final question. What do you know about the Sheridan sisters? Why was Jane Georgiana chosen as the Queen of Beauty? Why her, my darling, and not you? Write and tell.

WHAT A HORNET'S NEST I seem to have brought down on my poor head! I had no idea that you were quite so irate about the elevation of Jane Georgiana Sheridan.

Of course, I do understand, as you say, that once Charles had agreed to be King of the Tournament there was no question of your being anything else but the Queen of the Tournament by his side. And very distinctive you were, too, Vane, to judge by the caricature in Richard Doyle's book. I adore the green umbrella over your emeralds.

So the matter of any rivalry – yes, yes, I see – was entirely out of the question. The choice for the Queen of Beauty, the premier position at the Tournament, would undoubtedly have been yourself, had not the circumstances made any such prominence unfortunately impossible.

It was, therefore, a second best, alas, a poor Irish lady with a rather witty and illustrious playwright for a grandfather, who was dragged from her near obscurity in Bath or Somerset to do the honours, and receive the homage.

I only met her once, I must confess, though I knew the two sisters very well some years ago. I see Helen Dufferin from time to time in the country, gawky still as the years pass with her freckles and those teeth. But she has a remarkable wit, for a woman.

It must be a hard cross to bear to be thought, as they always are, the Graces Three. The Norton sister, I would say, is quite the equal of Jane Georgiana.

I used to be there at her salons in Seaham Place rather often in the early Thirties. One used to see Melbourne looking languid and alone in a corner, or pretending not to be bored with his partner on a sociable. Such dry, Whig elegance!

I was taken there once by Bulwer in my canary waistcoat days, when I was still recovering from my travels in Turkey. I used to have headaches that started in my toe-nails and travelled until they could go no further at the top of my skull. There they would stay, and frolic, until I was half-mad with pain and dizziness.

Aye, dizziness. I might well have accepted the attribution, as did the Earl of Sandwich the title of originator of the bread affair we all now eat, since the frail condition was one, I swear, that I suffered from far more than other people.

It led me to Bolton, later, and his consulting-room. But in those days I was forced still to endure the pain and pretend an indifference. Only Caroline Norton, I believe, knew what I was going through.

She would come and kneel on the floor beside me, and lay her cool hand on my brow, and look in my eyes with a sort of half-puzzled, half-conciliatory gaze, as if she was truly sorry she couldn't do anything to alleviate the ache.

Never for long, though. Or not if Melbourne was in the room. For all his coolness, they say he was quite a jealous lover in his older age. And he had the power at the time to exercise his feelings.

Well. For someone jilted by Byron, and led such a merry dance for years on end thereafter by a madwoman, I don't suppose that his later behaviour was too extreme, or too hard to excuse. He may, I like to think, have seen me in my oiled ringlets, and with my silken handkerchiefs, as a form of Twenties poet, a combination of minor novelist and unfailing seducer.

At any rate, he toyed with his claret, and turned his fingers, and inclined his head when we were introduced, and claimed, on what authority I know not, to have heard a good report of my *Contarini Fleming*. Which is more than ever I did, Vane.

'So what are your plans now, Mr Disraeli?' he asked, with a genial smile. 'Another novel? Or a long poem, perhaps? They say the day of the epic is not yet over. Consider Southey, eh? Consider Tom Moore.'

'I propose', I answered, aching in head and heart, I fancy, and nursing a morsel of uneaten chicken in my lap, 'to go into politics, My Lord, and to become the Prime Minister of England.'

I tell you, Vane, he was quite disturbed by this reply. He had supposed I was only interested in literature, and this was a shocking revelation. For someone dressed like a gigolo in a play to be thinking of entering the House of Commons! And playing there, if he could, the senior role.

'No chance,' he assured me, all emphatic, and very insistent of a sudden. 'The post is promised, as near as it may ever be, to Stanley. Stanley, you know, must have the job. Yes, you may go into politics, and I wish you well, young man. But Stanley will be the Prime Minister.'

So that was that. He ignored me for the rest of the evening, and I receded into my aching head, and my dreams of power, and my plates of cold meat, and my dull muddy wine. And my occasional conversations with Caroline Norton, the attentive hostess, but no longer, I was sure of that, the prospective mistress.

'A whore in her glad rags', you call her sister, Vane. But was she? Twenty-nine years old, I was told, and never a look for any but the future Duke of Somerset when she was the Queen of Beauty. And 'a paltry, insignificant little ninny'. Well, perhaps.

But Alford said that Jane Georgiana Sheridan could crack a joke like a tinker drunk at his daughter's wedding. And that she put up with the famous deluge, skimpily sheltered under her brother's crimson brolly, rather better than most of the other ladies.

Be fair, Vane. I confess that I like much better your tale about her cookery prowess. Is it really true that her most admired recipes are based on the broiling of the lowly guinea-pig? What fantasy!

If only Charlie Lamb had known. He could scarcely have stooped below his gonfalon to do his homage. It would have been much as if Lord Melbourne had found out that our Queen Victoria was a cannibal.

You have never tasted such dishes, you claim, but Lady Bouverie has eaten them roasted with almonds, and served in a sauce of rosemary and mushrooms. Delicious. It brings the tears of laughter to my poor eyes here in the dusty winds of our Paris October to think of Charlie Lamb as the Knight of the White Rose compelled to munch on a haunch of Lord Peter Ploughwright of Plumblossom.

No, I can scarcely believe it. You have used, Vane, your imagination. You have made her out more monstrous than she can have been. A sow and a swine, as it were. A positive Circe for the Odyssean champions of the sward.

I am resuming, as the colour of my ink will indicate, after a short interruption. George Smythe has just called.

It seems that things are advancing quickly. Plots are afoot, and matters of consequence are in the wind. He insists, and who am I to disagree with the son of a Duke, that the moment is ripe for a meeting of all our party, and some agreement on aims and immediate action.

'You must meet again with Manners, Dizzy,' George insisted. 'And make up your mind about Milnes and

Baillie-Cochrane. We need to be more than two, but not, I believe, more than five. When the session begins, we must have some identity as a group. With a flag, as it were. And a manifesto. And you, of course, as our leader.'

Heady stuff, my dear. They are all resolved, like conspirators, to be very secret, and to have a plan of campaign, and to meet – here is the nub of the matter – at Smythe's house in Gloucester Gate for a thrashing-out of the several details.

'You are bidden, Dizzy,' said Smythe, very serious for a change in his brown ulster, and his long gloves. 'You must come by the Channel packet on Friday and join the claque at my house on Sunday afternoon.'

So there it is. I shall be in London. And very soon. And entirely, if I may insist on this, incognito. Mary Anne will remain in Paris, here at the hotel and on her social rounds.

She is privy to all my plans, and fully agrees I must go alone. I shall scarcely put on a black mask and assume a false name, but, apart from that, my travel must make no stir in the news. I shall quietly sail from Dunkerque, and land in Dover, and post to London, and put up, for a couple of nights, with Smythe.

And so, providing, and oh, how I hope this will still be so, you are there at Holderness House, and propose to remain in London for the remainder of the month as you stress that you do, before Charles drags you back up north to wreak havoc on all your pheasants, then, Vane, we shall meet!

Meet, yes. And for the first time in nearly four years. I am highly excited. The very idea has put me into quite a cold sweat. I shall pause once again, to wipe my brow, as my grandmother used to say. That is, to make use of the chamber-pot.

I have been a martyr to a strange condition which is going the rounds, and has been given the name, by Colonel Barbaud, of the General's Welsh nanny. It seems that it makes a leap, and takes you into its arms, as the lady in question was known to do, and will only release you, in a much reduced state, after several days of acute indisposition and dire servitude.

I slave at the pot. I knead my muscles. I pray to the gods of the French latrines. But to no avail. I must do my time. And Mary Anne, poor woman, must do the same.

Let us hope, dear Vane, that the voyage will set me back on my feet. That, or the vile powder that I am prescribed by M. de la Corte. A physician, or shall I say a Torquemada, from Nantes. But the local sufferers all swear by his powers, and so I must try.

So. This is Tuesday, and George returns to London, bearing this letter in his bag. You will know, therefore, of my plans, dear Vane. And in good time, I hope, to make any arrangements that may be needed.

Of course, I can hardly hope for an answer, before I must leave. I place my fate in the lap of the gods.

Au revoir, mon amour. Until soon.

So. I AM BACK. From the heights of Elysium to the depths of darkness. The weather, dear Vane, has changed. November has Paris very much in his watery grip.

I gather from Mary Anne, who is relaxed, I may say, and rather having profited than the opposite from my absence, that autumn storms have been the daily rule during the five days I was away.

There are signs, indeed, of some weakening in the lead of the hotel roof, and maids nightly tour the upper corridors with bowls and buckets to catch drips. Our modest hostelry has endured these harsher seasons with frequent complaints, but the deluge is still, I report, held at bay.

I hope so. Even as I write, in house-robe and slippers, lying prone on my sofa, I hear the patter of French heels, and the suppressed giggling and urgent whispers I know to be the concomitant of a fresh attack.

Outside, the rain appears to be merely a thin drizzle – from what I can see, reared up on my elbows. Men in cloaks trudge with gloomy brows about their several occasions. But indoors, I suspect the worst. Infusion. Leakage. Water, as it were, along the brain.

Dear Vane. How different from those hours of dreamy sunshine through which we meandered in the woods at

Richmond, and then along the river bank, and heard the Wright family with their Sunday concert!

What a lucky spell it was. You were wise to invite me over to Rosebank, and to guess how little time there would be. I had no idea that Smythe and Manners would require so much of my energy.

I have been reading through the letter you gave me to carry on the packet, and made me vow to hold unopened until my return. I was faithful, my sweet, unto your instructions, and the envelope has been slit, and the sheet removed, no more than an hour ago.

The scent of your powder lingers. It brings those happy moments very close.

I dined at Brooks's on my last night in London, and fell in with Waterford. It appears that Lady Louisa has been busy sketching all the peasants on the estate at Curraghmore, and has got him keen on redecorating the village church in the vein of Pusey.

I never saw a man so changed. Where, I thought, is the old rollicker who stole the flogging-block from Eton and was claimed, according to Alford, to have used his groom's boys across it in the way of Hadrian with Antinoüs? Where, indeed?

It took several glasses of cold hock, and a fine cigar from my cherished reserve, to renew his interest in former scandals.

But then the eyes of this evidently only partly reformed warrior lit up across the loo table.

'I'll tell you a tale of Charlie Lamb, Dizzy,' he said. 'Picture Charlie, noble, slender, elegant in the stirrups, at speed along the pressed sea-shore, over casts of worm and scatterings of shell, a slayer of tiny crab and a scarer of prancing sanderling and itinerant cormorant. I ask you to picture him, Dizzy, as he might have been painted there by Etty, or perhaps by Haydon.

'The morning sun is low on the horizon, rising in frail carmine splendour above the trembling sea. A few fishing boats bob far out on the waves. A boy is mending nets in the distance, a dog is barking as it chases the birds.

'All is coolness, clean, free, open. There is romance in the air and on the wave. It is warming the blood of Charlie in the new sun.

'Then, lo, Dizzy. A vision. Some thirty yards away, as the horseman slows to a walk, examining some piece of driftwood on the sand, or tangle of bladder-wrack, a young woman, a mere chit of a girl, no more than in her early teens, is wading, calf-deep already, into the salt and unplumbed ocean, in the direction of the Witherings.'

He told the story awfully well. I was quite on the edge of my *fauteuil* there in the club. The blue haze of cigar smoke dissolved, the idle chatter of racing and politics was dispelled in a rush of pure air and, yes, there I stood, shivering and excited, on the bare sand at Bognor.

'She was fully dressed, I gather, Dizzy, and paying no attention to the soaked condition of her skirts or stockings. She was just wading forwards, out to sea, as if absolutely bent on self-destruction by drowning herself up to the neck in the waves.

'Charlie, of course, was amazed. Over the flank of his mare Clorinda he came. Down to the sands on light feet. Then at a quick sprint across the intervening space. And up to his thighs in icy water as he ran to stop the girl, halloaing to her as he went.

'"Please don't dwown," he said, or rather, Dizzy, I should say he says he said, for I have the tale direct, I may say, from the horse's mouth. "Wait a moment, won't you."

'And then it seems she paused, and turned round, and her eyes were full of tears, he says, and she was the most beautiful young black-haired beauty you ever did see in your born days, and never at six in the morning off the beach at Bognor, with her wet skirt clinging round her skinny thighs and her long hair tumbling out of its grip on to her shoulders and straggling down below her waist far enough into the water to be turned under and sat upon.

'"It made an impwession, Henwy," he said to me. "It made a vewy considerwable impwession."

'Anyway, Charlie had her out of the water, and into his manly, cradling arms in no time, and they were soon sheltered under a breakwater and chattering away nineteen to the dozen.

'The facts of the matter seem to have been that young Charlotte had been working as a chamber-maid in one of those awful faked-up little boarding houses in Bersted, and one night an Indian gentleman, who claimed to be a Rajah, had knocked on the door of her attic room, and begun to murmur extremely indecent proposals through the keyhole, upon receiving no response to which, save shocked horror, he had threatened to return on another occasion, break the door open, and enact what he had suggested, should she be willing or should she not.

'So the girl – imprudent miss, you may say, Dizzy – had gone half out of her mind with fear and disgust, and had risen early and run down to the sea-shore and could see no other way out of her misery save by a suicidal stroll face forwards into the bosom of Father Neptune.

'Charlie, of course, believes every word. At first, he said, his thoughts ran very much on confronting the rapacious Rajah with his lewd behaviour, and challenging him to a duel. But Charlie, of course, is a man of the world. Wiser counsels prevailed. Many a man, both English and Indian, has chanced to whisper a sweet nothing or two through a keyhole to a lonely maiden without therefore anticipating the play of swords with a complete and interfering stranger. And Charlie's own reputation in these romantic liaisons was not of the most unsullied.

'So what did he do? He decided to encourage the lass – just fourteen years of age, as it soon transpired – to return to the hotel, pack up her few belongings, and elope with him forthwith to Beauport.

'There, by some process of explanation easy enough to engender with his libidinous father, Charlie had a room prepared, and the girl installed, a virgin – well, at any rate, a mistress – in a tower. Saved from her dragon, and by a shining, if also a lisping, knight.'

So there it is, the inside story of Charlotte Grey. I knew, of course, that Charlie had married last year, and a rather youthful stunner at that, with raven hair to her bum and a flashing eye, but I never heard until now the tale of how they met.

Have you heard any other version? Can you corroborate?

I must draw to a close. You will already have opened and read the letter I left in your writing-box. Forgive the less amatory tone of its successor. You will know how much of my skill for passion I exhausted in the earlier pages.

Dear Vane. We were scarcely circumspect. It would ruin a promising career, and a great hostess, if it were widely known what we have done. Still. 'Twas fun. And more than fun. I shall write again. *A bientôt!*

I HAVE JUST HAD a letter from Count Walewski about young Louis Napoleon. Poor fellow! It seems that he's having a rather awful time in his prison at Ham.

Of course, the place is comfortable – according to Walewski. Plenty of Empire sofas, and the odd writing-table or two, and space for a large bed and a stuffed mattress on which to practise his high jinks.

But they limit his visitors to a handful a week, and even those are thoroughly vetted to exclude any undesirable political elements. I gather he has to spend the chief of his time writing. Essays on the sugar question – which surely possesses us all – and a dissertation or two on how he proposes to run the country when he returns to power.

Consider, Vane, the awfulness of exile succeeded by the irksomeness of incarceration. Do you remember him in London? A very fastidious, if somewhat remote, young usurper he seemed to me. Always frowning slightly under his air of courteous largesse, as if he had a plot or two tucked away in the back pocket of his trousers, and an idea that you might be able to help him out in some detail of their execution.

He took Mary Anne and me up the river once at Twickenham. It was after some party – at Lady Bessborough's maybe, I don't remember. We were the last to leave for some reason, and there was to be a picnic on an island near Richmond.

'I am rather expert with the punting-pole,' I recall him remarking, 'and I shall be delighted if you will allow me to ferry you both to our destination.'

So into the bottom of the rocking punt we both stepped, rather gingerly, I seem to remember, with Louis supposedly holding the craft firm against the bank. Then down we sat, side by side, in the stern, Mary Anne with her parasol atwirl in her lace gloves, I with my Sunday cane dipping off and on into the water.

We were all three very jolly, flown with a certain gaiety of good wine, and in high spirits. There was much laughter, and even, perhaps, a little good-natured pushing, and pretending to shake the boat.

'You must sit still,' Louis insisted, as he rolled up his sleeves, and grasped the pole in both hands.

'Do you do this often?' I asked, more by way of making conversation, I think, than to put him off his stride. But it made him frown and tense his lips.

'Enough, Disraeli,' said he, and shoved the pole hard down to the bottom of the mud.

There was a loud sucking sound, a squelch and a plop and up it came again, with Louis teetering to keep his balance, and the punt shooting forwards at a great pace into the main line of the current, narrowly missing, as it went, a pair of rowing boats manned by dour, burly men in jerseys.

''Ere, watch where yer going,' shouted one, and the other, I fear, shook his fist. Alas, to be an Emperor in another land, and have no recourse against such casual insolence!

But Louis, after all, had had plenty of practice. He merely inclined his head, waved one hand, then resumed his grip and thrust in again towards the rear of the boat. Again we shot forwards, even faster, perhaps, this time than before.

'Help,' said Mary Anne, clutching her veil, and pretending to be afraid of being thrown back into the water by our sheer speed.

'Watch out,' I called, in my turn, observing a moored houseboat looming up at us as we seemed to swerve for some reason back in towards the bank.

Louis was quick to correct his direction, but evidently much less keen to reduce his pace. Which was very much, as you may recall, his trouble in politics as well as in punting. He might easily, in my own opinion, have avoided the disaster at Boulogne in 1840 if he had only been prepared to allow the propaganda for his cause to gain support more slowly.

But he wouldn't wait. In love and in war, one must always wait. There is a right moment, a time to strike and win. Wrongly chosen, one is plunged forthwith into catastrophe – marriage, lawsuits, death on the shore, abandonment in the political wilderness, what you will.

So it was with Louis Napoleon. And there he is, pinned down for life, it may be, in a draughty bastille west of Nantes, with no one to console him except – so Walewski calls her – *la belle sabotière*, one Albertine Vergeot, who comes in, ostensibly, to shine up the Emperor's shoes.

A far cry from Liz Howard, and the cushioned salons of St John's Wood and Finsbury Park. However. To return to my tale of the Thames.

Past the houseboat we steered, and then past another trio of punts, and then on upstream at a formidable skimming speed, the envy and the cynosure of all eyes, it seemed, and indeed for a few heady moments I really did think that our elegant young Louis, with his arms brown in the sun, and the sweat standing out on his forehead, and a future of dominion bright before him, was at last going to reach his goal and deliver us in safety on the sandy shores of Eel Pie Island.

Alas, it was not to be. Mary Anne, I gathered later, had

long since realised what was going to ensue, and had eased off her shoes, and removed her gloves, with a view to making the subsequent watery immersion less encumbering.

Wise girl. I was less prepared. The end when it came was swift. There was a sharp crunch, a creaking and a tearing sound, a whirlwind of inarticulate swearing, and then we were all three tossed unceremoniously head over heels into freezing water and tangling weed.

I went under like a ball of lead, surfaces blowing and sneezing, and struck out for land. Several yards ahead I saw Louis gallantly supporting Mary Anne as she waded through shallows to the shore. There were willing, if rather angry and amused, hands to pull us all out, and in due course, after a good deal of money had changed hands, and profuse apologies been given, we made our progress to our destination in a hired ferry, under hands more skilled in the manipulation of oar and pole than our exiled Emperor's.

We made a melancholy and shivering group, and were entertained with iced sherbert, alas, and cooled white wine, and a great deal of chaff, and mocking talk. Which Louis, to his credit, I may say, absorbed in a very decent and friendly spirit, and not at all like a Frenchman.

Today, by the way, is the 1st of December. The snap of winter is in the air, and the Pomeranians are all out in their woollen jackets. They make little frosty powder puffs when they bark in the wind.

Winter, of course, brings Christmas. I saw the King again last Thursday at St Cloud, and he talked of nothing else.

'Mr Disraeli,' he said, 'I adore your English mutton. I would love to eat mutton instead of horse for Christmas. Yes, horse. It is always horse. They call it veal, or turkey, or guinea-fowl, but I know it is always horse.'

Curious, Vane. He goes on about equine matters like an Irish country squire. I admire his eccentric ways and his collection of clocks. But he is hardly the sharpest of wits, or the most determined of monarchs.

Talking of Christmas, I have begun to think of what I should like as a present. You may rest assured, though. I require nothing expensive, nothing indeed that is at all material. I request merely information.

First, since this is my Louis Napoleon morning, you must write and tell me about the notorious moment when the Emperor had to be restrained in his Ayrshire joust with Charlie Lamb. They say – or rather Waterford and Alford say – that there was real blood shed, and proper bandages brought to wrap the pair of them up.

Now, what was the matter? Who was to blame? What subtle scandal – political or private – led the two of them to lose their tempers as they galloped alongside each other in the rain? I need to know. Write and tell.

I have my own ideas, but I shall value your confirmation. Which brings me – can't you guess why? – to the lovely, lascivious and so indiscreet Liz Howard.

She was pointed out to me more than once, at the Eyre Arms and elsewhere, and so you can skip her tight skirts, and her golden stockings, and her loose long red hair, and her little breasts bouncing like peaches at Hallowe'en under her corsage.

I know the look of her. But we never – alas and alack, I say – we never met. So I want your candid opinion, Vane, your considered judgment as a woman of the world, of what it is about her that held the attention of two men as various as Louis Napoleon and Charlie Lamb.

Not, of course, to mention her original mentor – Major Martin, was it? – and then – dare I breathe the very idea of such a liaison? – the Earl of Eglinton himself. Had she bright ideas? Was she a wit? Is she still alive? Has she died of grief? I mean, for her sweet Louis in prison? Or is she waiting in lonely sadness, or – more likely – in salacious abandon, until his release?

You will know the answers, I have no doubt, or – at worst – will have the time and the opportunity to find them out. Let these be my Christmas present. And in return, here is mine. Guess what?

We are coming home! Well, not immediately. But Mary Anne is bored with the social round, and the English are trailing away, one by one, already. We can't, of course, be back until at least the middle of January, because I have work I am engaged in for Thierry, and it can scarcely be done at Grosvenor Gate.

But by the third week of the New Year, and some considerable time before the beginning of the session, I shall be home in London. With leisure, I hope, and with passion, to hear in detail, and *in situ*, and in *déshabillé*, and in desperate ardour, about the manifold elements of the world upon which your intimate knowledge will cast a fresh and, I trust, somewhat lurid light.

So tell me your plans. Where will you be? Is it Holderness House, as I eagerly desire, or – as I abjectly fear – is it to be one of your icy fastnesses in Wales or Ireland that you propose to winter in?

At worst, you might invite the two of us down to Mount Stewart, or Plas Machynlleth, or wherever else it could be, for a visit. We do at least know how to support our sherry glasses in unshaking hands and chatter about the Welsh rarebit or the Irish whiskey as well as most of your other society guests.

Be good, Vane. Take a risk. Invite Mary Anne down and bury the hatchet. You will find her quite excellent company. And, after all, there is hardly another way we can manage to spend much time together when you are at home in the country.

Unless, perhaps, I might assume a post as your gardener, or your amanuensis, or your private masseur. The last, I imagine, might suit my skills and my tastes the best. I am poor with flowers, and loathe dictation. But I do tone muscle well.

SO HERE I AM at the King's Arms in Dumfries, with a gloomy, low-beamed room above the courtyard, and a new candle burning in the holder to light my labours at the writing-table. All exactly as predicted.

I am not, I confess, in the very best of tempers. The gammon steak for dinner was as tough as the sole of an old riding-boot, and the apple pie had the texture of a soaking dish-rag. However, I will praise the cheese. A fair wedge of staunch Cheddar, and a brace of Abernethy biscuits to set off its flavour.

My fellow-guests include a distiller from Perth who was anxious to sell me a case of malt whisky at some improbably reduced price, a traveller in whalebone stays, who had the impertinence to ask if I was married, and, if so, what my wife's measurements were, and a rather mysterious, quiet individual who eyed me like an officer of the New Police and is employed, I feel sure, by some secret agency of government to watch my movements.

There was mixed conversation, as you may guess. I was glad to leave them all stooped over their beer and tobacco, and grope my way up the winding stairs to this rather smoky little attic.

Tomorrow, fortunately, I shall be up with the lark, and

off on the stage to Sunderland ere any of the three be out of the covers. At least, I hope I will. I could hardly bear the company of Dr Silence across the stormy moors to Northumberland. He would try my patience.

As for Old Whalebone Stays, he would soon be wanting your own dimensions, my dearest Vane, you may be sure of that. My intentions on this clandestine journey across the spine of England shine forth in every lineament of my face, and I have no doubt that the lecherous corset-vendor would be wanting me to furnish my luggage with a suitably constricting and lascivious present.

Enough of that. We shall be undoing each other in no time at all. Which is why, you may think, there is little point in my forwarding only a few hours in advance this harbinger of my eagerness, this gossipy and apologetic letter.

Well, you have only yourself to blame. You did insist that I write more often. Besides, I agree with you. I have indeed been remiss. Our last weeks in France were atrociously hectic, what with the concert at the Luxembourg given by the Duchess Decazes, and the Turkish soirée at the Odilon-Barrots's, and the assembly at the *Hôtel de Ville* given by the wife of the Prefect of the Seine. I could extend the list of our social commitments for a page or more.

Strange. The very act of announcing our departure seemed to make us twice as much in demand as before. The letter-opener never seemed to be out of my hand.

I could tell you all of this when we meet, on a sumptuous couch at Wynyard, or strolling with you in the teeth of the wind through some stripped laurel bower. I could, yes. But I prefer to dwell on the prospect of more amorous chatter rather than these dry tales.

Amorous, or none, perhaps. 'Mere lip to lip, in lasting silent thought. As in a dream of everlasting bliss.' You must help me with my blank verse. I am always at my best as a poet when I am in love.

Lord love us. I hear the step of the whisky distiller on the stairs, and I much fear he may see the gleam of my candle under the door, and suppose me up, and knock on the panel for a last word, and a final offer, on his way to his lonely pallet.

No. From his gasping breath, I think he is either drunk or on the verge of a stroke. May the Lord preserve his spirit, if not his soul. I see from my hunter that it lacks but a quarter hour until twelve, and the candle has a good length of untouched wax there to burn.

Good news. I feel very alert, and anxious to give you an immediate account of my entertainment at Eglinton Castle. The distiller, I suspect, is the last to bed, and I should have a clear run till the small hours, if I so desire, without fear of interruption from man or beast. Well, there was a very dubious cat licking her saucer of cream in the parlour. But I think I may say that an errant husband on the tiles is a match for any feline, Manx and tabby though she be. So here I go.

I have my doubts about whether Eglinton was as keen to see me in Ayrshire as he insisted in Paris. After all, I suppose that a rising politician who arrives well after the stalking season, and without his consort, and with little interest in billiards, or the breeding habits of Highland cattle, is not exactly the ideal house guest for a melancholy Saturday and Sunday in January.

Still, he did his best. I must put him down for a most hospitable host. He fed me with excellent lamb, and drew on the most exquisite resources of a fine cellar of claret. He walked me all round the policies, and I may say that the view of the grounds, and the lake, and the bridge, not to mention the distant, now grown-over space where the lists were arranged, and the tents of the knights pitched on the grass, all this made a deep and considerable impression.

He showed me the house, too. And I allowed my imagination to speculate – though not with too much difficulty – over which of the many bedrooms you must have discarded your own jewelled satins in.

Indeed, I unpacked my bags in my own remote, lofty chamber, with the supports of the four-poster rising like old oaks on all four sides of me, and I lay awake and listened, wondering whether it was the past or the present I was hearing in those nightlong bickerings that I picked up echoing through walls and along the turns of each vaulted corridor.

Was it the ghostly quarrels of the past? Or was it the more substantial altercations of the present day I was hearing? You may make up your own mind. I will tell you this, however. Lord Eglinton has a ferocious virago on his hands in the shape and person of his new wife.

A bitch, for certain, of the first water. An ill-favoured, short-tempered, ungainly, jealous harridan of a woman, if ever I saw one.

Dear me, I thought, when I kissed her hand. The powers who punish our sins have laid a heavy penalty on the errors of the 13th Earl of Eglinton. And serve him right, so some would say.

Farewell, it must be, at any rate, to whatever peccadilloes the good William was hoping to pursue alongside his more correct matrimonial observances. It was clear enough that no ogling of any wenches in church, or prolonging his clutch of any pretty cousin's fingers, or fondling the shoulders of a servant-girl, would be tolerated or condoned by the fair Theresa.

I was very glad that Mary Anne had been left behind. On me, at least, the grim widow cast no jealous eye. But I overheard some snatch of talk in the scullery, as I passed by on my way to the ha-ha, about how she had put a razor to her throat, and breached the skin before Eglinton got it from her, when she heard that he had offered a lift in his carriage to a village woman of fifty.

So there you have him now. The hen-pecked husband, the cock of the Tournament with his wings clipped at last.

However. It failed to spoil what was otherwise a most

informative and illuminating visit. I trod the field, I breathed the air, I was even, and to my not undisguised amusement, wet by the Ayrshire rain.

Did you know, by the way, that the castle was designed almost entirely by Eglinton's grandfather? When the old fellow inherited the estate, and came to the title, he had spent his life, so it seems, in a rather unambitious way, what with a bit of soldiering in America, and making some mild improvements to his estate in Coilsfield.

Riches and title seem to have been seized by him with a firm and exuberant hand. He raised money, he began to build a new harbour at Ardrossan, he hired an architect to amend the ancestral home. Then he sacked this hapless fellow and drew up his own plans.

What we have both now slept and undressed in, and one of us been, well, *had* in, Vane, as we both know, was erected at immense cost, and at a rapid speed, and with all its fashionable Gothic twirls and crocketings on a solidly classical and symmetrical basis, as recently as 1797.

Now there was something I never knew before. I had had the impression that Eglinton had been reared in an ancient mansion going back to the days of the Border Wars. Not so. It was all flung up, in brown freestone, on a small bluff, with an artificial lake in front, no more than fifteen years before he was born.

Moreover, the Montgomeries were the first bend in the line of blood for over five hundred years. This domineering, bow-legged little grandfather, who locked young William up with his aunt, and fed him candy, was the initiator of a new branch.

No wonder William felt the urge to emphasise his antiquity with something so glamorous and eccentric as a mediaeval tournament. Which, of course, he has very effectively done.

The thing that struck me most in our tour of the house, as you might expect, was that huge, four-storey octagonal hall going right up into the lantern of the tower. It was freezing cold, of course, in spite of the log fire they keep burning, and the travelling rugs that William insisted we wrap around our legs as we sat with our wine and stared up into the ceiling.

'Those are the banners, Dizzy,' he said, and sure enough so they were.

I might not have noticed, if he hadn't pointed them out, fraying and tattered above the decayed oils of his forebears, and the arrays of swords and targes. But there, indeed, they were, the colours and the shields of each of the thirteen paramours, hung up for all to see, and, emblazoned on plaques of mahogany, in bright gold, beneath them, the names of each of them.

'Alford, Beresford, Cassilis,' said Eglinton. 'Craven, Eglinton, Fairlie. Gage, Glenlyon, Hopkins. Jerningham, Lamb, Lechmere. Little Gilmour and Waterford.'

He ran them off, I may say, a bit like a roll of honour, as if they'd been slaughtered fighting the French on the field of Talavera. He spoke with more than a touch of reverence, though I must admit that the echo there in the hall could have added an extra and unintended solemnity.

'Fourteen names,' I said, for the sake of making some conversation. 'You put your own in, too, I suppose, to avoid any blasphemous hint of the good Lord and His disciples.'

He had the grace to laugh at that.

'My dear old Dizzy,' he said. 'You should put us all in a sonnet. A touch of Michelangelo might well be suitable.'

So we got up, and paced the stone flags, and I paused to admire a bust of Cicero – about the only Roman detail the house has left – and then we went on to inspect that frowning billiard-room where the guinea-pigs made such a nuisance of themselves on the green baize.

'Tell me, My Lord,' I said then, as we gazed out across the distant hills, very formally, as befitted a serious matter, 'why didn't you add the name of Louis Napoleon, too? Surely as the Knight Visitor he deserved his place?'

'Well, now, Mr Disraeli,' says Eglinton then, mocking my formality, 'I could scarcely write the one name NAPOLEON up on my wall, now could I? My father served with the Duke of Wellington, and died at Alicante. And the Duke is often here as my guest. It would really never do.'

The candle begins to gutter. I must be drawing to some kind of conclusion, and settling down on my little truckle bed. It really is, too, One of those low, flea-bitten-looking boxes with a fancy quilt thrown over the edges to hide the worm-holes.

I might be better staying up. I could raise mine host, I suppose, and demand a lantern, and make a stroll through the early morning streets in search of adventure, or perhaps, more probably, some boring stories of the town's most famous resident.

They say that Mrs Burns lived on in the wee house they now show to the public until only six or seven years ago. I paid my penny and saw the relics yesterday afternoon. A few books, a lock or two of hair, a pair of waistcoats. The usual clutter.

I hope if ever I become famous, Vane, that my heirs will put on show a better display of my life and foibles than the Burns children have done. Where, oh where, I found myself asking, is the sense of that lovely wayward poet of 'Tam o' Shanter'?

Not, at any rate, under that sandstone rotunda with the sculptured plough that holds his bones in the local churchyard. He deserves a more glorious, and a more witty, memorial than that. As I do, Vane, a more comfortable, and spacious, bed than this.

Until tomorrow, then. Good night.

10

You will be surprised, no doubt, to see the headed stationery. Yes, Ashridge. I can scarcely imagine what led me to subject my poor nerves to another dose of this execrable Lincolnshire Alford.

Well, I can, actually. I was foolishly duped into supposing that a few days at a house party with Peel and Bentinck present, to name but two, would surely promote the advancement of my sadly flagging career.

Besides, I was keen to view yet another of Wyatt's sham Gothic castles. In the course of which drear and Romantic pursuit, I had hopes of some further conversation, occasional, and sober, on the finer points of the sexual jousting in Ayrshire.

I have been much deceived. As for the masters of what we are still, I hear, to call the Tory party, my confidence is at a lower ebb than ever. Politeness, yes. A nod over the rolls at breakfast, an arm on the shoulder in passing through to dinner. What more could I ask?

I could ask a little serious discussion on the price of bread in Lancashire, and the prospect of the miners 'playing', on which you were good enough to give me your own, alas, Vane, rather prejudiced opinions at Seaham Hall.

Nothing, however, has been said. I watch them talking in

their low, conservative voices like so many Whigs at one of Melbourne's levées. Not a hint of passion or concern or any understanding of the country's problems amongst the lot of them.

If only Smythe or Manners were here! I feel like – which I know I am not, as the new session will show – a young insider without friends or party or following. But let them wait. You shall see, Sir Robert Peel. I have a rod in pickle for you, and the means to thrust it smarting right up your abominable, precious nose.

There they go. Off to build a snowman in the ride, with Alford in their wake billing and cooing over his new-boiled one-year-old. As bright red and babbling a babe as ever I saw in the four kingdoms.

These rooms, by the way, must surely be the coldest in England. A dessicated little maid brings up a small scuttle of sea-coal at eight every morning, and this, dear sir, dear little maid, is the sole allowance I have for the day.

So I must either sit crouched in my travelling-coat, with a pen or a book in my gloved hands, and shiver my way to perdition until the gong sounds for tea or mulled claret, or scramble down the draughty stone stairs to the courtyard and practise an invigorating dance on the cobbles while the other guests joke on about the rick-burning, and the deportations to Australia.

I am grown very radical. Very radical indeed, my dear Vane. In the mood I am in today, I would willingly see every brace of this fan-vaulting torn down by a mob of Chartist rioters, and the Alford family dragged out in chains to the tumbril and the guillotine.

Have you deep snow now, by the way? My heart yearns for those graceful colonnades of yours in Wynyard and the view you must have of the frozen lake from the pleasant steam-heated reaches of the gallery.

Why on earth the English aristocracy is so pig-headed about improving the means of keeping their houses warm, I have no idea. I have gone on about your systems, and your economy of coal by the use of water pressure and piping, but Alford is as deaf to the boons of the Industrial Age as his eighteenth-century powdered and periwigged father.

'Log fires, young fellow. Log fires, and a brisk walk in the morning. That's the ticket.'

Thus said the 1st Earl of Brownlow, when I put my point to him in the saddling-room. No time for steam, no time for coal. All he wants is a fallen tree and a hot saddle and a woman to keep him company. As the old ballad says.

Charles, I must say, has become as enlightened as Newton or Galileo under your expert guidance. I was amazed to see his interest in machinery, and in the subtler points of the stoking apparatus. I shall never forget the sight of Lord Londonderry in his frilled sleeves under a metal basin like a bath-tub with what I believe the polite newspapers would call 'an oil-dispenser' in his hand.

You are lucky, of course, with your coal. Not every landed family is so fortunate as to live within twenty miles of one of the most productive seams in Europe. Even if it does mean a rather squalid journey in a wheeled buggy to see where the glistening stuff is mined.

I hope you will not be too hard on that luckless overseer who left the paint wet on your seat, and thus ruined your cashmere shawl, and your winter dress, and no doubt your woollen underbloomers as well, if the turpentine be as penetrating as it seemed on the walls of the trucks.

Ah me, your temper then!

'I never want to see you again,' that's what you said, if I remember correctly, 'as long as I live.'

Memorable words. Which I trust will never be spoken in the heat of passion to your dearly beloved and most dutiful Benjamin D.

Who is desolate without you. And misses your deer-park, in its light dusting of early frost, and your dressing-room, in its light dusting of evening powder. And your screens from China, and your fans from France. And your giggling maids. And your far-away, tinkering, mechanical-minded husband. And your sweating, heavy, soft, belligerent hams.

Mmmm, yes. Those most. Those most of all, my dear. You reminded me, in your best moments, and may I single out amongst those the afternoon of the 19th in the laundry room, or the late morning of the 21st at the lonely coal face, oh yes, then most of all, the long night of the 22nd in the locked orangery, under the tartan plaid in the shade and the scent of the tropical palms, you reminded me, I say, of the most versatile and expedient of Turkish harlots.

There. Take that thought with a hot towel to your morning bath. I know your needs, my dear. Loose talk, and loose ideas. Those do the trick.

And after all, with no attentive Dizzy, rubbing the stiff places in your shoulders with oil, or changing clothes with you in the primrose bedroom under the chandeliers and the gilt mirrors, watching your breasts multiply a thousand times in the distance, well, with no attendant paramour, no rising politician at your beck and call ... how can you manage? How can you do the trick, Vane? How can you bring it off?

I see you lolling back, satisfied and replete, with a glass of chocolate, and a bowl of *petits-fours*, and a whirlwind of cushions lifting you high enough to look out across the cedars towards the sea, and the flakes falling, whirling and falling, as if one of the pillows has burst and filled the sky with the scraps of a million torn-up love letters, and you have plucked one, just one, down, and are lying naked reading the words, 'I love you, Dizzy, I love you, Dizzy, I love you, Dizzy'.

So sleep, my dear. And dream. Dream that I am lying beside you, caressing your hips. And perhaps your lips with my lips. And telling you all about my delightful journey back home, lonely though it was, from Manchester to Euston on the new railway line.

Do you know it cost me only fifty-three shillings for a place in a first-class car? All done up in Post Office black and red, and the seats upholstered in button-down leather, with an embossed fringe, and a padded headrest. I felt like a real Lord, I can tell you.

There you sit with your three companions – and mine were silent and unobstreperous enough to become part of the decoration – and the landscape flits by at twice the pace of a trotting mare, or so it seems, with a glorious plume of smoke, like a stallion's tail, afloat in the sky to one side.

The motion is very even, not at all the bumpy vibration which I had feared, and to which Mary Anne and I were subjected by the Teutonic railways on our honeymoon in Germany. There have been improvements. Most effective and luxurious improvements.

Why, there is talk – according to one of my companions, a distinguished old solicitor from the look, in a dusky coat and pince-nez – of a corridor from coach to coach, and a man passing by with a tray of hock and sandwiches.

No need for a bursting bladder either, he assured me, with a a word in my ear. They speak of a carriage with a close-stool, and a jug and basin to wash your hands in to boot.

'Railways, young man,' he murmured, 'those are the stock to put your money in.'

Well, he may be right. And I might follow his advice, if I had the cash to speculate with, which I don't. So I pass the tip on to you, my dear Vane, should you fancy a second string to your collieries.

Touching which – your collieries, I mean – I believe that your notion of starting blast-furnaces for the smelting of iron is an excellent one. You have an opportunity there, you know, to do more for the good of your tenants, and your employees, than a hundred hand-outs of Christmas game, or Easter butter.

Start a furnace, equip an iron-works. Your local iron-masters are the work of English capitalists. All self-made middle-class men, with flat vowels, and no more concern for the good of the country than a fox for a yard of chickens.

You are the mistress of the land, the wife of the squire. The industrial changes must come, I see they must. So let them be engineered by the traditional masters of the means of production, the landed classes.

You have nothing to lose, need fear no loss of gain. You are rich enough to develop with skill and with care. Fortune is already yours. Be her mistress, and use her benefits. Let the poor eat, and the sick be tended; the unemployed work, and the despondent lift up their hearts.

Here endeth the lesson. I see the snowman-builders return. Peel there in a long ulster, like Frankenstein in the novel, and Herries at his heels, like the monster itself. Alford with the squawling babe in his arms, pointed like a shot-gun directly up at my window. I can hear the brute scream like a trapped shrew.

I shall have to bustle. Mary Anne will be in soon from her sketching trip with the ladies. A few crayon drawings, *à la* Crome, of the south buttress, and a picturesque addition of a cow or two in the corners.

My fingers are likely to break off with the cold. I have even taken, at times during the composition of these lines, to the occasional striking of a lucifer to warm my skin.

Oh for your furnaces, oh for your boilers and pipes of steam! I am warming my hands in the recollection of your hospitality, your passion, and your hot rooms! I would give one of my frozen thumbs, I do believe, to be there in your boiling winter-garden, amidst the orchids. The other thumb would still be enough to do its work for you. Be sure of that.

Well, downstairs, in my rusty jacket, and frostbitten trousers, for a skimpy dinner, and a dry chat with Alford or

Peel. Orange Peel he is, that must come off, ere the fruit be eaten, and the juice enjoyed.

No more. I hope the repairs go on apace in the burned-out wings. Amazing it was to see how fast your men had repaired the ravages of the fire. 'Let Wynyard rise once more! Three-winged as once she was. Warm lady of our north.'

You see. I am a poet still. Write soon.

YOU ARE QUITE right to reprove me for my language. There were, as you say, certain passages in my last letter which might very well have inflamed the fires of righteous indignation, had but the uxorious Charles, your lord and master, laid his wiry hands upon them. Or his outraged eyes, for that matter.

But you are discreet, my dear. You know you are. That little enamelled casket with the silver key, which, when it travels – as it ever does, when you do – travels incognito, and amongst a ruffle of furs, and shawls, and under a mass of silken petticoats, and in an American trunk, why, that little casket, I do aver, will safely retain the most lascivious of my proposals, unseen, unmeditated upon, and without the good Lord's interference.

I am just as discreet with your own, admittedly much more cautious, epistles. Why, I read your latest, scented although it be, my dear one, with Nuit de Macao, in the total security of my lonely drawing-room, at four o'clock.

Mary Anne is taking tea with a friend, some West Country madam, with gossip of Cornwall and the state of clotted cream, and I know the doors of the green parlour will never open before the clock with the bronze putto strikes on the six.

Thus I am free, and alone. I put my feet up on the sofa, and I warm my hands before a roaring fire, and I sit like a Regency bachelor in his own rooms, coat off and sleeves unbuttoned, over a glass of the best Madeira.

Conning. Yes, conning, if I may use the old-fashioned word, the latest letter from my delightful and much-missed mistress. However, I must urge myself on. Having criticised my tone, you ask for information. And exactly as I would wish, and as you promised to do, in the character of my confidante and amanuensis.

The meeting at the Tower of London, therefore. The great assembly of the intending paramours, prior to the Tournament, in Sir Samuel Meyrick's gallery of armour on the 17th of October, 1838. What was it like, you ask? Who was there? Describe the room.

Imagine a Gothic cloister then, say a hundred and fifty feet in length, as long, longer perhaps, than your ballroom at Wynyard, and more than twice as high, with a hammer-beam roof, and a series of lower vaulted chapels. And in each of the chapels, mounted on an armoured horse, one of the chain-mailed and accoutred champions of English history.

Kings and dukes, earls and princes. They made a most splendid line. Like silver ghosts they were, in the haze of tobacco smoke, when the intending jousters had all arrived. Indeed, what with the flags and the cartouches of weapons, and the shields and the wooden plaques of arms, it was very much the perfect embodiment of what the prospective knights had come for.

'Order, order,' I remember old Meyrick saying above the hubbub, and banging with a sort of auctioneer's gavel on a table set up under an awning at the end of the room. 'Your Graces, My Lords, gentlemen.'

Then there was a dying away of the laughter and chatter, and a bit less jostling and striking of matches and general coughing and shuffling of feet. I must say it was very much the effect of a lull at a party, when the host insists on making a speech. A certain bored indulgence, and any amount of secretive glancing at watches.

Anyway, there was Eglinton, decisive and reticent at the same time, every inch the old Etonian amongst his cronies, and anxious to give a lead and yet not to seem to be very much bothered about what came to be decided.

He spoke rather briefly, and to the point. He proposed to hold a tournament at Eglinton Castle, the following spring, he thought, and he wanted as many of his friends and acquaintances as cared to equip themselves with armour, and a retinue, to come up and take part in some form of jousting.

Then someone called from the back of the room, a burly lout, whom no one seemed to know, lolling on the breast-plate of a German baron.

'My Lord,' says he, in a drawling tone, 'will there be a purse of gold, for a prize?'

From the general murmur of response, it was clear enough then that a fair number of those present had the idea of a competition for gain in their minds, and were interested in dipping their beaks, as it were, in the proverbial Eglinton riches.

'Why, sir,' calls Eglinton, with a smile at Meyrick there by his side, 'the remuneration is hardly the point. We shall fight, as most of us race, I hope, for sport.'

This was well received in some quarters, with Waterford, I remember, raising a vociferous cheer, but amongst the majority there was clearly a fair deal of dissent. So a wide-ranging discussion broke out, and there I stood – a few yards from Samuel Pratt, who was wringing his scaly hands, and hissing, whenever he disagreed with anything – and I lit a long cheroot, and I thought how like the House of Commons it all was, only rather more confined to the subject of debate.

I had gone along, as you know, in the way that a number

of others had done, rather fired with the notion of taking some part, and also in the mood to enjoy the rare spectacle of the aristocracy of England, or at any rate some large swathe of the younger portion of it, in a disputation on its own history.

As it happened, there was a vast ignorance of this. A handful of antiquaries, with Meyrick as the chairman giving some lead, revealed the depth and extent of the general confusion.

'You must choose your century,' said Meyrick at length, brandishing that silver gavel of his. 'And there are at least three broadly different sorts of tournament you may have.'

'A tournament for a bag of money,' called out the man lolling on the breastplate, who had emerged as better informed on the history than some others. 'Or at least let the beaten knights have their armour taken, and returned on payment of a ransom fee.'

'Their bodies, too,' called out another young sprig, jerking about like someone with St Vitus's dance under a drooping standard embroidered with gryphons. 'I say let's have a twelfth-century mêlée, in chain mail, and may the strong of arm prevail.'

I must say that neither he nor many of the other willowy creatures who seemed to have come for fun or wit looked at all likely to emerge as victors in this kind of combat. It was undoubtedly one, however, which had many supporters – purists, mere thugs, and, of course, men with debts. I saw their point.

'The law would intervene,' said Eglinton, very firmly. 'There is really no question of a simple struggle with sharpened lances, and a finish on foot with swords. It would be taken for a mass duel, and it would be stopped.'

After that, the floor cleared a little. About a third of those present walked out, and that was the end of the movement for a real battle, and real reward. At the other extreme, there were those who advocated an affair of silken lances, and ladies with favours, and a sort of Elizabethan masque, and a mock assault on a Castle of Love in an artificial lake.

'I say restore the courtly style of the last of the tournaments under King Charles I,' said a serious young fellow with a huge pair of whiskers. 'No violence, and no false reminiscences of mediaeval combat. Let elegance, and a nice frivolity, be the tone.'

He, too, alas, got short shrift, and he, too, and his party passed away. The room was beginning to look rather sparsely populated when Charlie Lamb rose, at a nod, I thought, from Eglinton and read out a long speech he had carefully written on a scroll of parchment.

'All gentlemen', he intoned, raising one hand for silence, 'must engage in plate armour, and on horseback. And in the manner, say I, of the time of King Henwy VIII. That is, at the tilt. With a bawwier. And with arms of courtesy.'

There was a good deal more in this tone, and plenty of yawning and eye-closing, I can tell you, Vane, and then Samuel Pratt, python-like as ever in his funereal black, was up on a plinth, and waving his hand to catch Meyrick's eye.

'If I may propose a resolution, Sir Samuel,' he rustled, very quietly, and yet like a box full of tissue paper with a poison fang in it. 'Let us accept Mr Lamb's excellent notion on a show of hands. I may add that my own humble establishment in Maddox Street will be happy to facilitate the Tournament by enabling all those who participate to obtain their equipment on loan, and on very reasonable, and special, terms.'

This piece of shrewd business allayed many fears of expense, and the show of hands, about sixty pairs by then, I suppose, showed a handsome majority of nearly two to one for the Lamb proposal. The meeting broke up, and some forty potential knights left their names on a list as firmly intending to participate in the tilt.

But you know all this already. It's the facts behind my

state of mind you want to ferret out. Now be honest with me. That's what's in your mind. I know it is.

Well, I'd come in from Bradenham. On the stage from High Wycombe, and all alone. With my father bent over his curiosities in the library, and his old eyes getting worse and worse through so many years of close print and inadequate lighting. And Sarah there sewing, and pouring tea for him in the afternoons. And the chestnuts falling in the Park, and the mist rolling up out of the stream.

But who else was there, you ask? Now, Vane, you know the answer to that. It wasn't Lyndhurst, and it wasn't Clara Bolton. That was long over. You know it was.

You think it was Mary Anne. In fact, you know she was there, and you know that I've told you why. George Wyndham Lewis died in March, and she didn't recover quickly from all that she felt about that.

My father invited her down, and she was the guest of Sarah as much as of me. I made her welcome, yes, and I spent much time in discussion of Maidstone, and the several political issues arising out of poor George's death.

Be sensible, Vane. Be fair. After all, he was more than just my partner in the constituency. We had many projects in common, and she was the heir to his papers. I had to be much in her confidence. Whatever happened between us, of a more romantic character, was of a later development.

I remember your great ball at Holderness House in August. All the doors open, and the candles burning in the chandeliers till dawn. The heat never letting go, as if the summer meant to destroy the difference between night and day. And everyone wet with sweat and peppery with powder.

That little room beyond your boudoir with all the mirrors. Louis-Quinze, and a pile of cushions, and you plumped up in the middle of them, like a Boucher cupid. The door bolted, and half your clothes thrown off, and the black mask left on so that you might have been anybody.

Do you suppose that I was enamoured of Mary Anne with the memory of nights like that in my mind? Why, Vane, I went to the Tower of London to be *your* knight, and to make some figure in the grand world that would take *your* eye, and keep you mine.

You know I did, my darling. So brush that jealous pout off your lips, and smooth that angry frown away from your brow. We were lovers then, we are lovers now. Mary Anne was once a friend, she is now a wife. She was never a rival.

I shall write again, with more in this vein. The fire is in need of logs, and the footman fails to answer the bell. I must gird my loins and go about the business of the house.

I AM TEMPTED TO admit you into another secret chamber of my experience. The enrobing ceremony. Or shall I call it, more correctly, the trying on of our armour?

It was one of those blustery, skirt-swirling March days when the weather isn't sure if it's on its way into spring or away back towards winter.

There was dust in the air, and scraps of paper flying everywhere, and a general shiver and clatter and fluster about the streets. London was in a fuss and a bustle. And Samuel Pratt's in Maddox Street was a haven of refuge, a storm centre in the typhoon.

We had all agreed – that is, the thirty or forty still interested in taking part – that the final date for the Tournament would be in the autumn, and not in the early summer, as was at first envisaged.

At any rate, the plan was to fix on a firm occasion when every knight had been measured and fitted up with his accoutrements. We had given ourselves over, at an earlier date, to the mercies of tape and ruler, and the dobbles, for such is the name for those humped, heavy dummies that hold armour, were now groaning with their metallic burdens.

I arrived at the shop a little after noon, with my mind on

luncheon, of perhaps a chop or two and a spice of cayenne pepper, and I found our splendid Samuel like a boa constrictor tied in a knot by a contortionist.

All twist and wriggle, and slither here, and rustle there, and stab and dip of nose into this room, and fork of tongue, and spit of venom, into that. The knights were a bewildered herd of rabbits, fascinated and stricken dumb, most in their underclothes, in long woollen leggings and neck-vests, or overborne and clanking in unsuitable steel.

Alford was out of sight in some awful closet, from which I could hear his petulant squawks and intolerant yells as a deft assistant attempted to cram his pudgy thighs into a pair of inadequate cuisses. Waterford was leaning on a vaulting-horse, or some fortified fifteenth-century equivalent of this, tossing a dagger up and down and catching it by the razor-sharp end.

'Eglinton,' he was saying, 'you look superb. I wonder, though, how you can move under all that weight.'

William, of course, was already encased in his golden suit, like a man on whom God has melted a hundred-weight of sovereigns, and left them to cool. Only his head, abnormally small and bony-looking, like the raw neck of a tortoise, was protruding from the glittering plates. It was smiling, immensely proud of itself.

'Only eighty pounds, I would say. Give or take a few ounces, Lord Waterford,' I heard Pratt slinkily interpose, 'and the weight is balanced, so that the man who carries it all can feel very easy. Is that not so, Lord Eglinton?'

But Eglinton made no reply. He put one hand on the vaulting-horse, flung up his leg, and had levered himself into the saddle with an elegant and unaided motion.

'Bwavo,' called a now familiar voice, and there, my dear, was our mediaeval expert and adorer of guinea-swine, the benevolently dusky Charlie Lamb, with a bottle of hock in his hand, and his chest enclosed in a coal-black plate of curving steel, like a pouter pigeon.

It was very much, to my own male eye, like the scene at a cricket pavilion, before the teams have dressed themselves for the game, and with pads and bats in evidence to take the place of our shields and swords.

But then you will hardly, I fancy, have glimpsed the bared bottoms and the hairy thighs of two dozen lusty men flicking themselves with towels, and larking about, in the aftermath of a challenge on the greensward with bowling and bails.

Imagine, rather, a giggling afternoon at your dress-maker's, with women of all ages, and their maids and female attendants, trying on new skirts and hats in a chaos of miscellaneous delight amidst the casual detritus of mirrors, puffs, powders, basins, ribbons, and all the other parapher-nalia of a girding-on session for the tournaments of the boudoir.

There were similarities, I am sure. But there were also differences. Men cracking men on the back with the flats of double-handled swords. Men choking on their gorgets, and signalling desperately to be eased out. Men posing before their tally-glasses, and turning brawny arms in their padded undersuits of fustian or leather.

The voice of Pratt. The presence of Pratt. The condoning hand of Pratt. The handkerchief up the sleeve of Pratt. The scaly tails, as they seemed, of Pratt, and the creaking alligator shoes. From lizard to snake and back, and from reptile to cold, crustacean crab, I admired his expertise, his ability to be everywhere at once, and his hissing charm.

'Your turn, Mr Disraeli, sir,' I heard him murmur at my side, and suddenly, Vane, I was no longer a spectator of this blood-curdling, bone-crushing affair. I was an active participant, led through a narrow door and into a small panelled, brightly lit room with a long cheval-glass, a table, a pair of dobbles and a couple of dry, grinning young men in shirt-sleeves with tape measures round their necks.

'Take off your clothes, if you please, My Lord,' says one,

a spry Cockney, and, 'he's no Lord, he's a plain Jew-boy,' says the other, supposedly *sotto voce*, I imagine, and in fact, I say, quite loud enough for me to hear.

So I stripped like a prize fighter, and further too. To my trunks, and beyond. You know how far, Vane. With those two supercilious dressers eyeing my circumcised parts like Burke and Hare, and then Pratt sliding in, and running a finger over my shoulders and round my waist.

I can guess they had trouble getting Alford into his chain hauberk after this kind of treatment. 'Try the bodice on,' says Pratt, and they button me into my arming-doublet, as warm and cosy a thick winter vest as you could shiver for on a cold day, and then, on top of that, lay on my shirt of mail, like a mat of silver chains.

They were quick with the sabotons, too. Over each foot, with my sole tickling, and then laced under the lift of the greaves at the calf. It was very much the heat and the itch that bothered me then, and I found it hard, Vane, I can tell you, not to be scratching away at my crutch.

'Easy now,' I heard the Cockney boy insist, and then, lo and behold, I look down and see I have iron thighs and two U-shaped poleyns – at the caps of my knees.

The rest was a rapid procedure from the waist to the neck, the laminated vambraces on my arms, the lumpy pauldrons over the shoulders. An hour, though, was spent on the sallet, or so it seemed, and the sense afterwards of being imprisoned in a steel cage, like a canary over a window, with only a tiny grille through which to see and hear the world.

'Gauntlets and sword, Mortmain,' I heard the remote, rustling voice of Pratt insisting, and then I had no feeling in my fingers, except for a sense of a great weight in my hand, and out I came, shoved through the narrow door and back to the main shop, with a faint sound of clapping, or laughter, and an occasional divided face lurching past my visor. Then a resounding clang, half the breath forced out of my body, and down I went on to the floor like Don Quixote.

Someone had the good grace to unlace my helmet and up I came like a fish blowing for air, red-faced, I vow, as an angry baby, and very much out of sorts and ill at ease.

'Dizzy,' says Charlie Lamb, 'you are one of us. A most parfit gentil knyght. I claim some wansom for your helmet. What shall it be?'

'A kiss, a kiss, I do declare,' cries the lecherous Alford, and then Pratt was there to the rescue, unlatching the breastplate, and offloading the gloves.

After that, I laid aside the undermail, and the padded suit, and stood round like half the others, naked to the waist in the heat of the candles, with my lower half all polished metal, and the middle a shaped mould in the manner of a cod-piece.

A lewd sight, you may think. And a loose, perspiring business, that brought on many a thought of a sweaty tumble in those close changing-rooms. I would readily, and I doubt if I was alone in this, have seen a bevy of whores driven in from Mother O'Riley's to squat in our laps, and feel our glistening thighs.

But no, there was none of that. Only the saurian Pratt with his tape and his frown, Pratt with his fondling boys and his mind on profit, and his thought on alterations, and making things fit. So after some talk, and a certain amount of slapping of backs, and being fitted again, and leaving fresh instructions, and all agreeing on the date of the 25th of November, the enrobing-session began to break up.

So out I went into the wind and the whisking skirts, and the flash of ankle, and flutter of bonnet, and round I went, after hailing a hansom – although I told you nothing of this at the time – to Holderness House. And there you were not, alas, dear Vane. And I left my card, and went off to the Park, and walked my passion away by the several lakes. And was home at last to my lodgings. And ate my lonely chops. And so on to the House.

I AM ALLOWING MYSELF an hour in the library of the Commons, behind a rampart of law volumes, the biggest and heaviest I could find.

The clerk is suspicious. He can scarcely believe in my new-found admiration for Blackstone and the History of Tort in the Middle Ages. But I shall fox his endeavours. I have a file of scribble set forth to my left, and an easy sliding position for the swift removal, if need be, of my incriminating parchments, that is, the sheets of my letter.

Your charcoal drawings of Costessey Hall, by the way, were quite amazing. It must be the most fantastical mansion in the realm. Old Buckler of Norwich, or wherever it may be, has done the Staffords proud.

When the thing is finished – oh, but 'if it were done when 'tis done', as the bard implies, then 'twere well it were done quicker – it will supply us with a history of the Gothic revival in epitome.

Strange how these vaulted manors, with their ivy-clad elevations, and their towers machicolated, or chopped away, or left half-ruined, strange, I say, how they all seem to have thrown forth some son of the Middle Ages, eager to accomplish his deeds of derring-do with lance or sabre.

Take Jerningham for an example. Here you have a second

son, with a small patrimony, and a stocky figure, and a look of his own middle ages already upon him. Why, you might say, should such a decrepit-seeming, and, yes, in actual fact, rather unathletic fellow be so avid for fame in a jousting-match?

No reason. Only the aura, the massive darkling shadow of Costessey Hall, brooding over his manhood as it glowered over his childhood, heavy with the echoes of modern masons, redolent with the spectres of mediaeval paladins, only this constant presence will explain his anxiety to go up to Scotland and sit on a horse and be shoved at with the brunt of a sharpened stick of pine, albeit cut on the cross-grain in the frail hope that it may shiver and fail to hurt or maim.

As you say, Vane, he was never a skilled rider. I saw him several times at the Eyre Arms, but not, alas, at the rehearsal you mention, when he did his famous tumble right over the neck of his mare.

I can well imagine you nearly splitting your stays. It isn't every day one can see the scion of a pre-Conquest family flung from the saddle by a tailor's dummy rolling on a trolley.

The Railway Knight used to get up quite a speed. You may not have realised in the stands how fast it could move on the iron rails, particularly when the wind was behind its back.

We used to spur forward, and the hunter would run at full gallop along the fence, and then on would come this inanimate opponent, with his painted silver armour, and his crude rocking-horse under his forks, and his mock lance up at an angle, and his egg-head, often bare of helmet, seeming to mock at all your pretensions, and then crunch, you were holding your broken spear, and the impact had almost hurled you on to the sawdust.

Others went over the neck, as well as poor Jerningham. Alas, too many. But none, lucky fellows, on the very day the cartoonist from *Punch* should have chosen to come. And so there he is, Vane. Immortalised for an accident that was common to all.

Was Liz Howard there, that day? In her usual place by the tents, with Eglinton and Louis Napoleon taking turns to pay their respects? I wonder. Not with you in the wings, I'll be bound.

She knew the times to be out of sight, that subtle hussy. Laughing with pot-boys like a serving-wench, and as coarse as a kitchen-maid when her paramours had their jealous mistresses in tow, or in view.

You would never have thought, to see her jest with a groom, or a cutpurse from Blackfriars, that she could be as delicate and refined as a court handmaid when she wanted to. She was shrewd in disguise. Knew the way to put women off their guard.

I saw her shake her red hair out, and lift her skirts, and belch like a street whore, when she thought the Duchess of Cambridge was harbouring wicked thoughts about her. But the Duke knew how she could lift that hair into a tall knot, and speak with charm about Fragonard, and swap names of the next Whig cabinet with Lady Bessborough, if she chose.

Now, Vane. You didn't know? But surely William ... Well, on my life, these men are so discreet. And I have seen her flirt her fan under My Lord's nose a dozen times in the provision tent. There was often talk of them seen arriving in the same wine-green berlin, too, for that matter. With the coronet over the door, and the curtains drawn.

But then, who cares? Those were free, licentious times. Now weren't they, Vane? More so than I supposed, in love and enchanted as I undoubtedly was. But then, times change. And lovers, too, perhaps.

Not us, though, Vane. Not us, eh? Now here am I, in the midst of a most serious debate on the future of the King of Naples, closeted in the darkest corner of the Commons

Library, and with what on my mind? What else but thee, my sweet, my heavy, wayward mistress?

Beshrew me, you say. That word again. How many times have I told you not to call me that, you presumptuous puppy? Alas, forgive me, my dear. I half-forgot. The other half, how could it ever forget?

We must wash again together. There is a pleasure I had never known before in covering an energetic woman with soap, and wrestling with her on a slippery floor.

But what of Charles? What, indeed? You never thought of that when I bolted the door, and you watched a thousand repetitions of me massaging French lotions into the small of your back. Narcissus, I think, was transformed into a woman that day.

As for your shocked little maid, with her pins and needles, and her tripping heels. I like to think of that fat butler – Soupçon is it, you call him? – catching her bent over with her outraged eye to the keyhole.

'What spanking then! What naughty squeals and firm descending hands!' I imagine a dry-point etching, in the manner of Blot or Darcis, for that scene. Our own, more indelicate, enactment, I fancy done in oils. A Dutch apostle of Rubens, good on hips. Bosse, maybe. Or van Bassen.

You see, I have been researching the right artists for our lascivious liaisons. The library has a special section, locked with a key, and opened only on request, for those members – the right word, one might say – who seek out such information in their spare hours.

Hence the implausibility of my current interest in the Law. Our noteworthy clerk has me down for a buck who comes in for his thrills. The revelations of the female flesh. The engravings of parts little seen in public. The privacies of the past.

So I have to go. He becomes restive. I shall take my screed and resume in the Park.

Your brush, by the way, pearly inlay and all, will return

on my next visit. I have it safe. Which is what I was about – when that interfering young Cockney with the stale cravat and the cocked hat interrupted my flow – to write.

The sun, poor fellow, seems very reluctant to shine this afternoon. I am stuck on a slatted bench under the shadow of a plane tree with an old woman eating peanuts, and feeding the shells – or so it would seem – to a coven of sparrows.

Let us hope that the birds grow not too ambitious. I fear for the inviolate white of my superior House of Commons ruled writing-paper. For Official Use Only. Do you hear that, you sparrows?

I was out at the Eyre Arms with Mary Anne the other day, on a drive towards the woods of Hampstead, and I felt sorry to see the decay into which the place has fallen.

The new landlord must look to his laurels. The veranda is in need of a coat of paint, and there are slates missing on the roof. The parapet is in poor repair, too, for that matter.

When we were first there in the June of 1839, a mere three years ago, after all, it was as spick and span as a newly commissioned fire-engine. All green shutters, and white doors, and the serving-girls in a pale blue livery, with clean aprons, and their hair done up under shepherdesses' caps.

There used to be a view from the smoking-lounge on the roof garden – and it was indeed a garden, too, with beds of gardenia and pots of Flemish roses – as far as the dome of St Paul's, and north right away towards Highgate, and some of the country churches.

I used to enjoy eating my soup and cheese there and looking down at the bouts in the four-acre field, where the lists were arranged. It was all very much of a toy affair, from that height. One required the assistance of a telescope to see all the detail.

Charlie Lamb, I remember, had a pair of opera-glasses on a silken thread, and he would sit in his dressing-gown – an elaborate, rather Chinese confection, with runic script on the revers, and a pocket for a fan – and stare down at the various jousts in the manner of a racing-tipster assessing the odds.

'Vewy good, vewy fine,' he would murmur, and then draw in his breath at some awful, or venial, misdemeanour of horsemanship or protocol. 'You mark my words, Dis-waeli. Captain Maynard will cawwy off the pwize.'

Of course, as we both know, poor Maynard went down with Egyptian gout, or some other imported calamity, and the dress-rehearsal was the last time his caracoles and his flaxen hair were seen. He had to withdraw, and the field was left open.

As for Waterford, the prime contender for the handsomest knight award, with Eglinton, of course, and my own good self rather close at his heels, dear Waterford took that ridiculous toss in the dung, and was face down in the shit, as they say, for a good half-hour before they could raise him up, and it took a pulley and crane, too, to complete the job.

He was pretty furious, Vane. Smeared in the ordure of the cattleyard, and with sawdust all over his metal jointings, like a burst-open doll in a metal travelling trunk.

The problem was that no one knew how to undo the plates, or at least not exactly, and once the brave knight was installed in his suit it was usually a matter of Samuel Pratt and his excavators, as afterwards they became secretly known, being there on call to arrange the unbuttoning.

On that particular day, it was Waterford's fault for being so vain. He wanted the ladies to see him ride a course in his full accoutrements, and so several of us helped him into his armour without the professional aid.

Very mercifully for romance and young love, Lady Louisa was absent this messy day. He had to swallow a fair mouthful of pig manure, I fancy, in order to get any air through the grille. His face was a study in faeces.

Lady Louisa could have brought her charcoal and

sketched a study for A Man Dishonoured, or A Lord In Disrepair, or some other moral tale. Very much in her vein, after all.

Fortunately, the dress-rehearsal went very well. There were only nineteen left in the field, as you know, and the Knight of the Golden Horn, alias Mr Benjamin Disraeli, was not of their number. Of which, as the talentless Mrs Gaskell would say, more anon.

The sun shone bright. After all, it was the 13th of July, it ought to have done. The Duchess of Cambridge looked regal in scarlet. After all, she is the wife of the seventh son of King George III, she ought to have done. The knights, resplendent in their several colours, performed with skill and aplomb. After all, they had practised for seven weeks on end, and they ought to have done.

I was there, of course, in the crowd. I mingled and saw it all. Two thousand six hundred and ninety, they say, were there. And all on the personal invitation, hand-written in a fine Gothic script, of Mr Samuel Pratt in person.

Not a cloud in the sky. Not a gloomy face to be seen. The Railway Knight on his best behaviour. The quintain whirling, arms out like a toy wooden soldier, and the knights taking their buffets in good part, and with perfect manners. Much shaking of hands, and little shaking of heads.

Except, alas, for my own. The dark, Satanic visitor. The Byron of the brave day. I went round with my long face, and my deep frown, and my carefully selected suit of entire black, right down to the gloves and cane, and not a soul seemed to notice, or bother to speak a word, and so console my sense of grievance, and my sense of the waste of life and time.

Not even you, my dear. You were off in Wales, passing canapés to the survivors of those mountain boar hunts, or is it bores at which they point their carbines? I can never remember.

Alone I was. As alone then in the thronging crowd as now on this griping bench, where I am treated, I see, to the preliminary attentions of these abominable birds.

Alone. Except for an old woman, and her bag of shells.

14

I AM IN MY STUDY, wet, windblown, and still in my outdoor boots. I am breathless. I am shaken. I have just poured myself out, and, alas, feel little better for, a massive allowance of brandy.

Why, you ask, all false concern, and womanly imitation of tenderness? Well, to put it bluntly, I have been robbed. Robbed, Vane. And in a callous, irritating manner, and in a public place.

Let me give you the full story. I had gone with Bulwer, after a dull session on the Chartists – and I sometimes think we shall never be done with the Charter – gone, I say, for a stroll beside the river, and to make a pilgrimage through the new Tunnel.

A marvel of engineering, no doubt. All massive round arches, and hollowed alcoves, and a sense of being like Jonah in the belly of the whale. Except, of course, for the mob.

I never saw so many people in my life. It seemed as though all of Stepney had come with his wife and family to patrol through this great snake of brick and cement, and to mingle echoing voices in a vast, unmeaning hymn of commentary.

So we jostled our way, elbowed, ousted, and impolitely

addressed, from one boring end to the other, and then back and out to the sunlight once more. But not, I may say, without first paying out our fee of one and sixpence for the privilege.

And not, and here is the nub, Vane, before some unknown assailant and vicious cutpurse had stumbled against my thigh, slung me against the wall in the press, and had his dirty fingers into my jacket and whisked my sovereign-case away.

'There he goes,' cries Bulwer, waving his cane.

'Stop, thief,' shout I, rising to my knees.

But where is the man with the money? Where, indeed? All that I see is a swirling mass of heels and petticoats, a chaos of pushing men and women.

Devil a sign of a policeman, despite the notices at the entrance about the patrols. Devil a sound of a whistle. Devil the grasp of a helping, official hand.

So up I get on my own, dusting off mud and sawdust, and away I trail, with Bulwer all solicitation and then irrelevant chatter about his play, which I think is his very worst, and the theft is reported at the station in Bow Street, and the officer will do his best, and has every expectation of apprehending the culprit, and a messenger will come to Grosvenor Gate as soon as there is any news, and so forth and so on.

You know, it was my grandfather's case. It isn't the money I worry about, although, God knows, that matters enough in itself. But the case with the Star of David meant rather more than a mere vessel for containing lucre. It held memories.

Imagine, therefore, my state of mind, on entering this haven of refuge, my private study – even if it does still contain rather too many echoes of George Wyndham Lewis in its Empire decorations – to find no fire, only a bare ashen grate, no friendly warming kettle of Darjeeling tea, only a cold earthenware pot and some floating leaves.

But instead, yes, a polished salver, with an unopened letter. A letter. Hmmm, I say. From whom, at this time of day? I turn it over, I settle back in my chair at the Carlton House table. I reach for my Cretan letter-opener.

A warm glow is passing through my chilled frame. A letter. Yes. A letter from my love. With what trembling, eager hands I slit the envelope, and withdraw – what?

Three pages, perhaps, of passionate yearning adoration? Two pages of cheerful chatter, and news? Even one page with a scrap of witty gossip, or a scandalous tale of a friend?

My dear, dear Vane. A simple, gilt-edged card, in a footman's handwriting, announcing your exclusive reception for the 21st of March, to which Lady Frances Londonderry would like to invite Mr Benjamin Disraeli. No other message.

Now, Vane. We both know. This is merely insulting. The matter has been discussed between us a dozen times – Mary Anne is very jealous. She always was. There are no circumstances in which she will tolerate or condone our friendship unless you are prepared to invite us, in common, and together, as man and as wife, to your public entertainments.

You know this, as well as I do. Your card is a prick, and a jibe. It hurts me. It stirs me up. This is hardly the day on which I can swallow the thing as a jest.

I have drunk another brandy, and taken a turn between my windows, and handled the mouths of the lions on the pier table, and I almost feel ready to write my reply.

Not, of course, only to this ridiculous *carte d'invitation*, which you may take as undelivered, or as answered already in the declining negative, whatever you will. I mean to your question, when we sat over our game of chess last Sunday, and you had my rook.

'Mate, I believe,' you said, and I watched the emeralds glisten between your breasts. 'You must tell me, Dizzy, exactly why, you know. But *exactly* why.'

Then you paused, and looked up at me with your angry, gigantic eyes wide open.

'Exactly why you married Mary Anne. And exactly why you married her then.'

So the merry-go-round was given a nudge all over again, was it not, my darling, and the question to which you, of all people, know the answer perfectly well, why, this question had to be put and savoured and slobbered over and insisted upon all over and over again. Did it not? And it wasn't your mate, now was it, or mine either, it was only one casual incident in a boring game that finally neither of us won.

I will answer, though. And in cold print, and for whomsoever may wish to read it. So. Let us go back to the spring of 1839. I saw you in the Park on the 4th of July, do you remember, and I raised my hat, and you asked your coachman to pause, and I climbed up into your brougham, and we rode through the dapple of sun and shade, watching the shop-girls with their cheap parasols, and the children playing on the grass, or being wheeled in their tiny carriages.

We discussed the Charter, and whether the Commons had been in the right to refuse to discuss the petition, and whether the million or so who had signed it were all suborned, or even real. Then we moved at a faster clip out into Knightsbridge, and away towards your milliner in Gough Street.

And, of course, we discussed the rehearsals, and how they were going. I told you about my horse, Pascal, and how he was playing up at the quintain. How I was giving orders for a golden horn, my emblem, to be woven in a pennant for my squire.

And I told you, Vane, and I'm sure you remember this as well, how my creditors were down on my back for a thousand pounds, and I had to have the money at once to hold them off. Or else I should have to withdraw from the

Tournament, and send all my armour straight back to Pratt, and have my deposits returned.

You listened, oh yes. I see you now as you listen, leaning out of the window, with your Chinese fan snaking to and fro in the breeze. We were passing Apsley House at the time, and I remember peering over your shoulder to see if I could spot the Duke strolling in his garden.

But, no, I couldn't. And no, you couldn't, either. Lend me the money, that is, when I had to ask in as many words. As you knew I would, as you'd always said you would.

It was never spoken, of course. We were lovers, Vane. There were things we never needed to put into words. And this was one. But the truth of the matter was always clear.

I was going up to Scotland to ride in the Tournament as your secret knight, and to bear the horn as our private colour and emblem, the horn of passion, and the horn of plenty. Why, we discussed it often enough together, and made our drawings of how it would look, with a certain curve, and a certain stiffness ... oh yes, my darling. Yes. Like this.

You remember well enough. And you remember, too, what you said in the brougham. Over your shoulder, and flirting your fan.

'Oh, I should ask your old friends the Austens – Austens, were they? – for a loan. It shouldn't be hard. They were always helpful enough before.'

And then the carriage was turning into Piccadilly, and you were nodding to friends in the street, and I was forced into what you know I loathed, a direct solicitation. A plea, for the money.

'I haven't seen either Sarah or Benjamin for nearly five years. It's out of the question to turn to them. I was wondering, Vane. Whether you ... ?'

Then the carriage was slowing to turn up Albany Street, and you were preparing to gather your things, and to have the door opened, and to go about your business at the milliner's.

'Why, Dizzy,' you said, all surprise, and casualness. 'I wish that I could, you know. But it wouldn't do. It really wouldn't do.'

And that, as we know, my dear, was the reason I withdrew from the Eglinton Tournament. And stepped down that day from your carriage, into the sun and the busy street, and lifted my hat, and was gone in a fury, and in a pitiless sadness, and knew that something had changed. Changed, and in a way that I didn't understand, or, yes, Vane, in a way that I understood rather well, but scarcely wanted to.

So that, then and there, walking down Piccadilly, and swinging my dolphin cane, I came to a sudden decision. I would marry, yes. After all, and against my plans, I would marry.

And whom? Well, who else but my old friend Mary Anne, with whom I was close, and knew very well, and who had money, and who was not unattractive, and with whom, well, yes, I admit the fact, there had been, in the past, some passages of arms. Not many, and not of depth, but some.

Yes, I thought, as I swung by the barbers' shops, and the glittering arcades, and the bow windows of Merry's and Benson's, with their great rounds of cheeses, and their parades of guns and hunting-bags, I would make a proposal of marriage to Mary Anne. And that very day.

So I hailed a hansom, Vane, and I gave the order, and I drove here to Grosvenor Gate, and I urged my suit, and I was accepted. And that, my dear Vane, was that.

'And when shall we make the happy day?' says Mary Anne, all ringlets, and rapture – you know how she is, Vane.

So it came to me, then. In a flash of ironic triumph.

'Why, the 28th of August,' I said. 'No point in waiting.

The day after the session ends, my dear. The day of the Eglinton Tournament.'

Well, there was Mary Anne, fiddling with her piece of sewing, and as delighted as a cat with a dish of cream.

'So you won't be riding in the Tournament, after all,' she murmured. 'What a shame! And so many of your friends will be up there, and unable to come. I hear that the Marquess of Londonderry is to be the King of the Tournament, and so Lady Frances will scarcely be able to attend our little celebration.'

Yes, Vane, imagine me there, or rather, imagine me here, cross-legged in a Louis-Quinze chair in the morning-room, and inspecting my nails, as if I had scarcely a care for that in the world.

'Never mind,' say I, seemingly insouciant, but, you may be sure, Vane, still seething underneath. 'I know Bulwer will come. And Lyndhurst. And the Montefiores, for sure. Who else do we need?'

She kissed me then, throwing sewing aside, and leaping into my lap. Need I keep my own counsel about that, any more? You know the rest.

We met at Rosebank, of course, a few days later and just before the dress-rehearsal, and I doubt if we exchanged four words in that silly crush in your long conservatory. You were far too much in your Marie Antoinette mood for my taste that sticky afternoon.

And far too much the coquette with our man of the hour, dear William, the 13th Earl of Eglinton. One could hardly get near him for newspaper men with their queries about the final details of the rehearsals.

But you did your best. To fob them off, and guide him along to your copper kettle and your China tea. And your little, gossipy conclave with Charles about the lists and the proclamation.

I stood with my ice and my champagne, and gnashed my teeth. And that was that. That, I mean, except for a few letters, and an occasional sight of each other across a crowded room at a ball. And except perhaps, I like to think, for a certain mutual yearning, alone in bed at nights.

Except that you, my dear, were never alone. There was always Charles. Charles, yes. At least, Charles.

Until now. And here we are back as we were, quite reconciled, and in love as before. And in lust as never before. And in good humour, if a trifle irate, with each other.

So Vane, enough. You know all about my reasons for marriage. And your own, too. I shall see you soon. I hope with my sovereign-case. They say that the Star of David should make it an easy object to recognise, and a hard one to sell.

But the Jews, as they say, have ways to melt and to alter. There are Israelites, alas, and some in my family, who would purchase a sovereign-case, and be pleased to have got their Star already emblazoned.

So I am not hopeful. But time will tell.

GOOD NEWS!

I was writing in my study at Grosvenor Gate only two hours ago when a messenger in a blue uniform arrived at the door, and, according to Fuller, who was not at all taken with his appearance, was most insistent that he 'see Mr Disraeli immediately'.

So in he was shown, and over he handed his official letter, dictated that very morning, *this* very morning indeed, and informing me that Inspector Goddard of the London Metropolitan Police was anxious to have the pleasure of an interview, when he hoped that he would have something to communicate to my pleasure.

I thanked the messenger, I gave him a shilling, which he declined. The police, it seems, are not now to be bribed, or accept reward. One strike for the puritanical Peel, eh?

Then I took my cane, called a hansom, and was over with small delay at the Bow Street New Police Station, a large stone building, a little like a Florentine palace, with a columned portico, and a green-painted, rather cavernous hallway.

Up I go to a high desk, to an immensely serious, grey-whiskered fellow in a helmet, with a large ledger in front of him, and a bottle of ink and several pens.

'Your business, if you please,' says he, eyeing my beige cravat with scant enthusiasm.

'Inspector Goddard,' say I, and then realise I have rubbed the magic lamp. No further introduction or message is needed.

A snap of the fingers, the emergence from a sort of hiding behind his desk of a thin, bony midget, and I amble along a rattling corridor to a door with a name on a brass plate, Inspector Goddard. A knock, and in I go.

Vane, he was wonderful. A plain-clothes fellow with a smudge-coloured waistcoat and a long coat and trousers, and the manner of being a sort of Duke's gamekeeper, which, for all I know, he once was.

'Mr Disraeli,' says he, extending his hand, and motioning me to a chair. 'A great privilege. Not every day that we encounter a Member of Parliament in our sordid, though I feel very necessary, business. No, indeed.'

Well, by this time he had a mug of tea poured, and a fairy cake laid out for me on a blue-flowered platter.

'In a short space of time', says Goddard, lowering his voice, I would swear, and looking around the room, as if for unseen auditors, 'I have every reason to suppose that the mystery of your disappearing sovereign-case will be solved. If you will bear with me, sir. A man will shortly be apprehended, and brought to this building. And should the case, as I anticipate, be found in his possession, then your assistance in making a formal charge will be much appreciated.'

So there we sat. I with my tea, and my Matterhorn of a cake. He with his formal manner, and his general conversation. Which, I may tell you, soon led to a subject even more fascinating to me than the background to the robbery of my property.

Do you know that Inspector Goddard, now the scourge and master-mind of a vast and intriguing department of policemen, was only three years ago a mere fledgling detective, and employed as a Bow Street Runner? In which capacity, with a senior colleague, one Ballard, now retired, he was summoned at the instance of the Ayrshire Constable to serve as a hunter-down of pickpockets at the Eglinton Tournament!

What a tale I now have to tell of the criminal underworld and its defeats and, alas, a few victories on the 28th of August, 1839! But first, the sergeant, I see, is clearing his throat. I have papers to sign.

It appears, alas, that there must be some further delay. The anticipated thief, one Cat Simmonds, who is thus called for the lightness of his tread, and the unusual fastidiousness of his toilette, has, after all, not been seized with the case on his person. A search is to be made, of his dwelling-place. And the Inspector would have me stay, if I will, until the outcome of this manoeuvre is known.

So here I am, with more tea now, and a better chair, and a fair supply of paper to write upon. The light is good from the high windows, and the table supplies as firm a surface as one might wish for. I shall press forward, I hope without further interruption, for over an hour.

Do you remember, Vane, as you sat there up in the leaking stands under your coroneted umbrella, if you ever noticed a rather surprising number of men in armour amongst the crowds?

No, not knights. Rather furtive, irrelevant-seeming men in armour, with their hands free of gauntlet or shield, and a tendency to be standing or walking rather near to those ladies with jewels, or sporting wallets of notes, or handling bags of money?

The fact of the matter is, astonishing though it may seem, that a handful of the most notorious of the London swell-mob, whose faces are well-known to the police, had the farouche notion of disguising themselves in hauberk and helm, and thus mingling unobtrusively with the throng.

It seems to have been forgotten that expense and inconvenience would limit the presence of the fully armed to a tiny few – and those mostly beside their tents and horses in the lists – and thus render the appearance of the criminals conspicuous, and make them easy to detect and apprehend.

'I was able', says Inspector Goddard, and with justifiable pride, 'to secure the most famous cracksman in England, sir. One Singlet Wilson, normally only to be seen in a thin shirt, and with bare arms rubbed in grease to make holding him firm an impossibility. The armour, alas, was his undoing.'

It seems that these armoured villains were all put upon a train, and returned to Ardrossan, later to be charged on the testimony of members of the crowd. Which the ensuing downpour made very hard to obtain. The majority, I gather, got off scot-free.

Far worse. According to Goddard, they sat down in their street clothes again in the saloon of the *Royal Sovereign*, and commiserated with the bedraggled survivors of the crowd, as they arrived in the evening, and bought them warm drinks of mulled wine, and plundered their persons to their heart's content on the voyage home to Liverpool.

'I was able, however,' says Goddard, with a grim smile, 'to put one or two behind bars. A local corn chandler, I am glad to say, was prepared to make a deposition about the purloining of a gold watch. Which happened, some weeks later, to reapppear amongst the private belongings of Mr Smalleyes Borrowdale, at his attic roost in Seven Sisters Road. I gather, according to the said gentleman, to his considerable surprise. You see, although I would never repeat this in public, Mr Disraeli, there is more than one way to kill a cat. Or to capture a known scoundrel.'

So there you are, Vane. Some secret information on the working methods of our successful constabulary. I fancy the Home Secretary would scarcely like to have Goddard and his gang brought up in the House against him.

But then, as Goddard himself knows, I would never dare

to make use of what he has told me. No evidence, after all. Bare allegations, and very prejudicial ones at that. 'Impeach the fellow!' they would cry. And a promising career would be in ruins.

'The fact of the matter is, you know,' continues Goddard, as we drink our tea together in that frowning, dingy office of his, 'that we haven't the forces at our command to deal with crime. A little here, a little more there. We stem the tide. We even press back the waters. But the fountain-head – if I may mingle my metaphoricals, sir – the fountain-head is beyond our grasp.'

So there I sit, shaking my head, and seeming to agree, and really not being at all sure as yet whether I am being made an accessory after the fact or an ally before the cataclysm.

'There is one man,' says Goddard, and this is where he actually lifts and extends a finger at me, Vane, 'one man, I say, or rather one monster of a man, whose evil genius is behind half the unsolved mysteries in the ledgers of this department. Murders, Mr Disraeli. Robbery. Vandalism. Assaults on women, old and young. Kidnapping and cut-pursing. Stab-wounds and face-carving. You name the crime, sir, however horrible, wherever committed, and you name the dark spider at the web centre who has had his finger in the pie.'

He had me on the edge of my seat with anticipation then, I can tell you. A novelist of some repute was lost to the world of letters when Mr Samuel Goddard elected to make his career as a police officer.

'Elephant Smith,' says he, spitting the name out, with a mouthful of cake. 'Elephant Smith. He's the man.'

You may well imagine what kind of fugitive from the freak show this alarming sobriquet served to conjure up in my mind. With reason.

'This Elephant Smith', says Goddard, marshalling his thoughts, 'has been so called for two reasons. He has the physique, to begin with, of an elephant. He is believed to weigh twenty-five stone, although no one has ever, I imagine, had the courage to invite him to stand on a pair of scales. His ears, furthermore, are enormous, and they hear everything. His ankles, too, are abnormal, both swollen, and of a rubbery texture. And he has protruding, yellowy, carious tusks, with which he tears at a bone of raw meat while he talks. And then his temperament. Like the elephant, he never forgets. Neither a favour nor – more particularly – an injury. There are men at the bottom of the Thames today who have reason to recall the long memory of the man they call the Elephant.'

Of course, I took all this with a pinch of salt or rather – since I had the box in my vest – with a pinch of snuff. We have lived through a brief age of deformitomania, Vane, if I may cadge a noun from our new humorous magazine, and Mr Punch has a point. Still, this Elephant seems, really, to be a creature from the pages of some Eastern legend.

'I travelled up to Scotland,' says Goddard, elaborating his portrait, 'on the second-class train from Euston. The 8.45, it was, with a place on a bench and a break for lunch at Birmingham. And better seated by far than those in the open trucks, third-class. But not the Elephant. He was rolling north with his whore in his own coach, with a specially strengthened springing, and four horses, at each inn, to draw the burden. They say, when he travels, he never shows his face, but holds it wrapped in a burgundy cloak, for fear of causing some fine lady to faint. We shall see. We shall see.'

At any rate, it seems that this master-mind of the world of vice was, indeed, at the Eglinton Tournament, unseen or no, and that his minions were directed in their nefarious endeavours from the Sultan's tent, as it were, of his curtained victoria.

While Goddard and his master Ballard were hunting like bloodhounds in their franklins' clothes, the wolf in person, or rather the Elephant, sat still and sly in modern dress behind his own windows, and, by the light of his own candles, fondled his woman and directed his operations.

Think of that, Vane. They say there is one criminal for every twenty honest men in this nineteenth century of ours. One Elephant Smith for every fourteen gentle knights, perhaps. Just think of this very one himself, at the heart of the lists, in the forks of the Tournament. I find it makes me shudder.

It seems that the sovereign-case has been found. With a basket of other gold and silver delicacies in the magpie's nest – that is, in the lodging-house that shelters, or once sheltered, Mr Cat Simmonds.

A wiry, wizened little man, he was. Not much above five foot two in height, and as thin and nimble as a willow-stick. Half-starved, I'd say.

Indeed, his condition touched my heart, and I was for letting him go with a warning; but the tortoise Goddard would have none of this.

'There is Crime to combat, sir,' he insisted, 'and this bewildered minion is a vital foothold on the ladder that leads to the monster Smith in person. Do a deal with him, as I may, before sentence, and there could, I say no more than could, be a thread to lead me to the centre of the – Labyrinth. Be firm, sir. Remember the poor babies choked in their cradles to force their mothers into his filthy stews. Driven to freedom and prostitution, and by dire bloody murder.'

I am back at home, Vane, and in my study again, and warm and comfortable, and I wonder what to believe. This England of ours is surely a foul place where the very guardians of our institutions are compelled into trickery and extortion to keep the Law.

Mr Goddard has given me food for thought. I shall turn over his views on crime and the conditions of life in the slums of the Whitechapel Road with care. Alas, he is no less antagonistic to my race than the creator of Shylock.

'The money-lenders are to blame,' he confided to me, as I came away with my case. 'The Jews lend them money, at exorbitant rates, and when the poor are forced to pawn, either clothes or their labour, the net of crime steps in – if a net may step, sir – and has them by the throat. You have written novels yourself, Mr Disraeli. Follow the path outlined by the master hand that has penned us *Oliver Twist*. There you see Crime well-limned. Well-limned, indeed.'

Thus. I have taken my leaf from the gamy pages of the Israelite-hater in person. But not, I think, oh not his deplorable prejudices. Nor Vane, those of the goodly Goddard, either. Who would see all money-lenders – but not one Christian Member of Parliament – as essentially Jewish.

HERE AM I, SEATED in my calf-length morning-coat, and my new puce cravat, at a spindly-leg satinwood affair in your salon, with a pile of your best Holderness House stationery, and a quill dipping in cochineal. At least, it looks like cochineal, to judge from the colour.

What on earth would posterity make of that? I can hear the sound of your voice from the other room, while you give instructions – behind a screen no doubt, lest I slip in unobserved and see you in petticoats – to your new Cornish maid.

Alas, they turn over fast, these girls. You are coy, and whimsical. They are prudish, or dilatory. I am forward, or nosy. Aye, they turn over fast.

Why do I write such imprudent, improper things? And why do I write them here, in your house, when I might, in a moment or two, if I so chose, rather utter them in person, and with all the additions of gesture and emphasis that the speaking correspondent enjoys?

Well, Posterity. Well, Vane. What fun it is for a moment to address one's remarks to a pair of attractive ladies, instead of only to one! The answer is clear enough, as we all three know.

For all my time in the House, and my skills in the boudoir

practice of eloquence, I am still a writer. And I enjoy the opportunity to practise. Particularly on such excellent writing-material as this hand-woven Italian octavo.

Ideal for the *billet-doux*. Outstanding for the intimate memoir. And a precious boon to the penniless writer of novels.

Is this one of those? I wonder, Vane. The preliminary skirmishes, no doubt. The sending forth of scouts to explore the terrain. The earlier encounters, even, with the enemy.

After all, one may write a book in a letter. Or at least in several. The epistolary style bears the accolade of respectability, and also, even better, of impropriety. *Les Liaisons Dangereuses.* We are certainly enjoying one of those.

And so. The room, Posterity. An elegant salon of the 1820s, decorated in gold and cream, with a looped fanfaronade of a curtain instead of a ceiling, to make it seem like a tent. Or a marquee, to be rather more grand.

Foreground. A young man – well, still fairly young – at a French ormolu writing-table. To his left, a harp. To his right, a jardinière, with a large Sèvres vase, and a quantity of iris flowers.

There are numerous windows, doors, etc. A classic representation with someone in a chariot, and a number of wolves and lions, in raised plaster, tinted in pastel shades, on a panel in the ceiling, appears through a gap in the marquee, like a scene featuring the Olympian Diana, on high in the clouds.

Enough. The sounds? Music, one might think. Alas, Posterity. No Haydn, or Mozart. Only the far-off, muted laughter and women's chatter which I have already mentioned. The hint of lascivious instructions and malpractice which the sound of a lady being dressed by her maid in a neighbouring room is always inclined to arouse in one's mind. The frou-frou of dropped silks. The rustle of stockings. The violin-twang of the plucked ...

No. I go too far. Not even you, Posterity, will allow me to speak so plainly. Not even you, Vane. In your dirtier moods. And so, to the scents. The aroma of roses, from crushed vials, although there are no roses in season. The sweet cedarwood smell of your cabinet of butterflies. The nuance – no more than this – of an arm perspiring, a sweating groin. A stink of lust. From where? Yes. The dimpled satin cushions of your double-ended *lit de jour* over there by the sewing-table.

Not that, oh no. Nor the feel of a trembling thigh, either, beneath a gloved hand. Nor the heave of a bosom under its bodice. No. Nor the taste of . . . Well. Is it apricots in brandy? Or a sharper flavour? Lemons in vinegar? Is it those on your lips today?

The virgin of St Austell has just passed in and out. Lifting your shawl from the back of a chair. Averting her long-lashed eyes from my frankly, Vane, very much admiring gaze. And removing her darkly glistening bulk of bombazine, like a little appetising pudding rippling on a platter, to your own, I am sure, less appreciative mercies in the dressing-room.

I am lustful, Vane. I am anxious for another go – if I may call it that – on the plumpened softness of the double-ended sofa. Reserving oneself has its disadvantages. One feels uneasy.

There. With the window open it feels a little better. The rough sounds of the street coming in, the rattle of carriage wheels and the cries of the lamp-lighters. The blood cools.

I shall pass my time – since I know you will bathe, and that takes ages, before you present your buttocks for another bout – in recording some notes of what you were saying.

It is a calm summer's night. The sconces are lit, and the servants bustle to and fro. Some matter of great moment is in mid-flow.

The carriages are all put away in their house, the wheels and the bracing oiled and made easy. The horses are in their stalls, heads in their mangers of exquisite hay. Far off, beyond the lake, the many-coloured tents are billowing a little in the light wind. Enough – just enough – to cause the pennons of their knights and masters to fly as horizontal as bright fish in a stream.

The long gallery in the castle has been cleared of sofas and set with a series of great refectory tables, laid end to end, and lit with a battery of magnificent scarlet candles. Footmen are in livery, serving-maids in the kitchens are sweating at their pans. The fires blaze, and the spits turn.

A vast roast, and a sequence of turkeys, and a plethora of hams and pies, and then more of the same – all suitably modern, and strengthening, and nutritious, lest any of the prospective paramours lose heart, or be incapacitated by sickness – a groaning spread of heavy meats and vegetables, and then puddings and fruits and cheeses and savouries, sweetmeats and liquors; all this, and not to forget the fluids, great flagons of red wine, magnums of champagne, jugs and pitchers of fruit cups, pots of coffee, carafes of water cooled in ice; all this, and then later, after the departure of the ladies, boxes and trays of cigars, immense Havanas, lit from torches, flaming and smoking like the blast-furnaces of the Sheffield steel-works, or the coal-burning smelting-works of your own Seaham Hall, Vane, as you aptly suggested; all this, eaten, digested, swallowed, drunk, puffed and scorched away, prepare the thirteen knights and the various officials of the Tournament for their labours on the morrow morn.

'The Burning Tower is on fire,' cries Waterford as he points a finger at the red-faced Francis Hopkins, who is either inflamed with claret, or blushing at an indecent story.

'Scorched by the dragon's tongue, no doubt,' replies Alford, remembering that Waterford is the Knight of the Dragon.

And so on. Swans that ought to be mute, when they talk too much. White Roses that may become hybrids, if they stain their petals with any more burgundy.

The candles flickering in their holders. The windows open to keep the room cool. The carcasses and the joints and the legs and the bones ravaged and gnawed and abandoned and left aside or borne away and replaced by others. The bottles emptied and renewed, the cigars unribboned and cut and drawn on. The clocks inexorably ticking the hours away till midnight.

I had it in mind. Even then. Even on the very day, as I sat up alone in my lodgings in St James's, with a dry streak of beef, and a dab of stale mustard, and a brace of rumpled apples to serve as dessert. Thinking of my own trials on the morrow, when the knot would be tied, and the ceremony performed, and the noose put round my neck, and with only Bulwer and Lyndhurst to be my supporters.

The condemned man in his cell at Newgate. Now what does he think before his execution, Vane? I wonder. As I did, maybe. Of brawny loins, and the white splash of semen. And then of breakfast, whatever he may desire. And then of the ritual, and whether his hair will seem brushed right, and whether his chin will hold itself straight.

I was early to bed, Vane. Much earlier than you, I fancy. Swilling your beaker of Mouton this or Château that, with your eyes on what you were after, and meant to be having before the night was over. Swelling there in its pouch of buckskin, and waiting, too, for its own epiphany. Its pythoness, and her coils.

I lay for a long time, I remember, with my head propped up and wakeful on my interlocking arms, and the moon outside making the whole little attic room dead white like a shroud.

The ghost of Christmas past. That's what I felt like on my barren truckle bed. The skeleton of a lost affair. The man with no future, only a drear procession of identical days, and a similar, bleaker succession of identical nights.

Identical nights, identical knights. In my own darkness, Vane, I visualised the paramours at the castle filing up to their lonely, separate and Gothic rooms. Twining in ones or twos, shouting a last good night maybe, or swaying on an iron banister, as they made their way up the huge circling staircase, like a cobra rising to strike, as it wound around and around the octagonal central hall where they would later hang and abandon their shields and colours.

A few would sleep alone. Craven, maybe, and Cassilis. A few with their wives. A few – like Charlie Lamb with Charlotte, her black hair down to her naked toes in the glow of the cheval-glass – with women or mistresses brought in, and later taken out, in a diligent secrecy. And a few, oh yes, a substantial few, Vane, with the wives of others.

The little cupid and ormolu affair with the jade and ebony on your mantelpiece is telling me to conclude, and leave you to your prolonged toilette. I think I may.

I am off in the morning to Manchester, and will write again from there. You know how to find me, if you should require to, with a letter to my secretary at the Midland Hotel.

Farewell, my sweet. I am folding the envelope, and licking the flap, as if it were the quivering nether lip I adore to moisten. Lewd fellow that I am. And so, to the door.

WHY DID I LEAVE so early? You know perfectly well why I left so early, Vane. You were much too busy with your dressing-room and your Cornish maid. As I thought I made clear in the letter I laid on your sewing-table.

Why on earth do we have to quarrel? I was handed your two sheets of abuse when I arrived yesterday evening at the Midland Hotel, hot and weary after a forbidding journey from Euston.

Really, my dear. What point is there in accusing me of abandoning you? You know my feelings. You have heard my professions of love. You have seen the enthusiasm with which I greet you at all our meetings.

Enough. Let us cease, please, please, to disagree about so many and such trivial matters. I look forward to coming back to London. I am eager to see and to touch, ah yes, to touch you again. My dear, you know I am.

In the meantime, the state of England is not what it was. I rode up, I say, in a train buzzing with speculation. My travelling companions – in the enforced awkwardness of a second-class carriage, I may add, owing to some fearsome blunder in the booking of my railway ticket – were all agog at the possibility of another march of the Chartists from Oldham to Manchester.

Now that I am here, and boiling in a stuffy room on the third storey of the new Midland Hotel, from which I have a fine view through the industrial fog over factory chimneys and desolate warehouses, I am well aware of the strains.

The north is another country. One-fifth of the population of Leeds is dependent on the poor rate. More than half of the master-spinners in Stockport have failed in the last nine months, and no less than three thousand dwelling-houses are untenanted.

There is neither capital, nor profit. The blast-furnaces of Wolverhampton are extinguished. The Sheffield cutlers can find no market for their knives. Here in Manchester, neither King Cotton nor Queen Iron are what they were.

The streets are full of a sulky, discontented, irascible mob of men without work, women without food, and young people without hope or energy. Something, Vane, must be found.

We need a new channel. A fresh water-course down which the old floods of investment may roll once more, unimpeded, relentless, and to the general advantage. But what can it be? Aye, there, indeed, is the question.

A man I met on the train – a local solicitor from the manufacturing town of Stalybridge – assured me that he had the answer.

'It must be the railways, I tell you, sir,' says he, breathing a fume of peppermint in my face, 'there is nothing else that will serve. Either railways develop, and at a speed unforeseen and unprecedented, until the country is one wide interlocking network of sleeper and shunting-engine, or this England of ours is a dead duck.'

He may be right. I have talked to several bankers here, and some men in the business of rolling-stock, and they tell me there are signs of a great shift. More confidence, more will.

We shall see. Perhaps in another ten years these idle cotton-weavers and shoemakers will all be shovelling coal into the boilers of steam-engines, or collecting tickets at the barriers of provincial stations. Ten thousand jobs, perhaps, and all for railwaymen.

In the meantime I am threading my way through crowds of beggars, handing out an occasional copper to the sullen, the dispirited, and the forgotten of God.

Your own miners, I wager, are feeling the pinch. How many have you had to lay off this last year? Five hundred? Or six? What is your famous coal to be used for, if the great engines of Bradford and Liverpool lie silent?

Alas, the great engines of the Ashton to Manchester railway line are already – albeit, I hope, only temporarily – silent. I am seated in an open-sided carriage in what, I believe, is called a railway siding, waiting for some obstruction on the line to be cleared.

What it may be, I know not. A goat, perhaps. Or a procession of striking metal-workers. The local tracks, I fear, have not yet achieved the high level of maintenance for which the London lines are famed.

So, I am still. The sun is shining. I perch in a drowsy silence on a worn bench, with my arm on the rim of the carriage rail, enjoying my view of a dank canal, and a straggle of poisoned willows.

No tents are visible. Not even one wing of Samuel Pratt's magnificent wooden stands, or the pine and creosote fence of the barrier, along which Charlie Lamb will charge, for glory and for Charlotte, tomorrow afternoon.

Poor Charlie. He turns. There in the four-poster behind him, naked except for a single petticoat, the last of her seven, his fifteen-year-old, although no longer virginal, mistress is bending to rub some cream on her navel.

Hmmm. I am dreaming, you say. Am I really, Vane? Perhaps. But elsewhere in the house, I know, and you know as well, my dear, there are certainly very familiar awaitings and entrancements and entanglements in oil, and not always those few specifically licensed by law, or custom. Eh, Vane?

So Charlie – yes, to be fair, let us keep to Charlie – kneels down at the foot of his little altar of armour, for, yes, he has mounted his full suit of equipment, like Don Quixote in his barnyard, on a trouser-press in his turret, and is intending a bit of a vigil.

No, not all through the night, for sure. There are other things to do. Sleep, for example. But, yes, for an hour or two. Well, yes. For a minute or two, at any rate.

And the pouting breasts on the crackling linen sheets behind him are pressing, almost, in imagined eagerness on the small of his back, as he fondles both sword and helm.

'Until tomorrow,' says he, in a low whisper, crossing himself, and stroking the polished steel.

Then he turns, Vane. Turns. And, oh Lord love a duck, Vane, what manner of thing is this that he comes bearing in his hands? A gift? Or a burden to suffer and to endure?

Oh, please, Charlie. Please, Charlie. Please, Charlie. Please.

There are ninety-one guests in the castle, and over thirty coupled in such a manner, at such a time, and with just such gasps and gulps, unfoldings and straddlings, clambering and seating, spanking and slapping, just such suppressed squeals, and such deliberate provoking, just such squelching and disgusting forcefulness of entry, such lingering and abusive withdrawal, just such bottomless love-making, between this one and that one, Lady and Lord, master and mistress, man, yes, at least once, Vane, man and man.

So Charlie ... Charlie, yes, with his little whore who claimed, so I hear, to be an illegitimate daughter of the Duke of Norfolk, lay on his massive, creaking bed and did his duty by all the priapic standards he had learned from his dissolute father.

Afterwards. Well. A furtive removal, by secret stairway, and in steamy underclothes, with a serving-man and his groping hands to show the way, a pair of horses champing at the bit in the stable-yard, an exchange of gold, and a closed carriage in company with a lax and sleepy young harlot, swinging through the back avenues to a booked room in a private house at Irvine.

Like so many others. A night of entrances, a night of withdrawals. The gravel never cooling from the heat of the horses' hooves.

And I, awake or sleeping, far away in London, Vane, the Knight of the Golden Horn, whose trumpet was never blown.

So Charlie ... Turning on his left side, and facing towards his armour, and the draped colours of the White Rose, fell into a satisfied, and a lugubrious, if weary, slumber.

In which. And now my imaginary forces work. I see Charlie dream. Dream, yes. But of what?

The moonlight drifts through the Gothic casements, and tinges the gleaming armour with snow, and makes the buckles wink in the great Saratoga trunk, with its freight of towels, and dressing-cases, and silver brushes, and shaving things, and the skeleton clock under its glass dome chimes the hours with a faint spinkle, and the body of Charlie Lamb, Esquire, turns in uneasy sleep.

And the Archangel Gabriel appears to Charlie Lamb, let us guess, in his dream. The Archangel Gabriel as a very large, and rather angry, guinea-pig.

'Now Charlie Lamb,' says the Archangel in a deep, sepulchral, bacon and pork fat sort of voice, 'I have a bone to pick with you. Wake up, and listen to what I have to say.'

So Charlie wakes, in his dream, and sees the Archangel there in a rusting suit of armour, crouched at the end of his bed, and licking his huge paws, with his large, grave head on one side.

'You may call me Plumblossom,' says the Archangel,

reaching down to the floor and lifting a leaf or two of a massive lettuce, as big around as a laurel bush. 'And you may remain as you are, in bed.'

For we may assume that our Charlie, being a creature of etiquette, is making some move to arise and perform a proper sort of bow to this unexpected arrival, even perhaps to get up and draw on his trousers, or at least his combination underclothes, and seem decent, and suitably chaste.

'The point', says the Archangel Gabriel, in his guise as a guinea-pig, 'is a simple one. You have failed, so I hear, Charlie Lamb, to believe in the existence of God. Oh dear, oh dear. Oh dear, oh dear, oh dear.'

And the Archangel shakes his whiskery face, and breathes lettuce at Charlie, who is shivering violently, and attempting to get a word in, at least edgeways, while his formidable visitor is pausing.

'Oh, Plumblossom,' however, is all he gets out, in a sort of choking gasp, and then the Archangel has begun again.

'Plumblossom me no plumblossoms,' he says, very solemnly. 'Or rather, in other words, be quiet. I have little to say to you, Charlie Lamb. I am here. I am the Archangel Gabriel. See me and weep.'

So Charlie bursts into tears – very sensibly, we may both suppose, Vane, in the circumstances – and is bowing his head in his hands. But the Archangel, though the agent of a merciful God, is disposed to make some sort of punishment an essential feature of his visit.

'God does not forgive you entirely, Charlie,' says he. 'But He proposes to be lenient. You shall fight in the Tournament tomorrow. But you shall lose. And you shall be shackled for life, in due course, to that faithless little popinjay you have just sent home to Irvine in a green brougham.'

At which, the moonlight wavers. The Archangel is a blur of fur now. He is on his feet, lifting his tail round his armour. He munches the last of his lettuce.

'Plumblossom,' he murmurs, as he begins to dissolve into a spume of mist, 'remember, Charlie. My name is Plumblossom. And God exists.'

Then Charlie wakes. Wakes, not in, but from, his dream. And remembers. And shivers. And pours himself a glass of brandy, and drinks it down in a single gulp. And falls off to sleep again.

A man with a chain is walking down the line, and the trucks are beginning to clank. I do believe that the engine is getting up steam again. So much for Charlie Lamb. So much for Plumblossom.

Well. I shall, after all, I think, be in time to hear Cobden speak. The Anti-Corn Law League are never prone to start at the hour they indicate.

Tell me – are the rabbits running in Wales? My regards to Charles. I hope you enjoy your hunting holiday. And so – with a puff and a jerk – we are off. To Ashton!

18

YOU MAY WELL ASK why so much time has gone by. Electioneering in Shrewsbury has kept me busy. Well, I call it electioneering. Eating steak and kidney pie with the Lord Mayor and his aldermen, and making all the right responses to their addled opinions about the Corn Laws. I certainly call it electioneering.

Without a smile here, and a responsive nod there, and an 'Oh, yes, I do agree, sir' and an 'As you rightly say, madam', I scarcely think I should return with the same majority as before.

Mary Anne has been a tower of strength. I know not exactly why, but the solid burghers have taken my darling wife to their humble hearts. There were cheers for her on the balcony of the Town Hall, and our procession through the streets to the bridge, after the Bachelors' Ball, was a virtual royal progress. With Mary Anne as the Queen.

I am very much, it seems, the second fiddle to her first violin. Still. It will bring in votes, and I must swallow my pique, and put a good face upon my jealousy.

This candle will hardly see me to the end of my page. I shall try another. There. A more even, and a better, light already. The room has quite a romantic air in a proper radiance, at least when one is on one's own.

You will gather that I am writing in bed. Very much like the Scrooge of our little Charlie's *A Christmas Carol*.

I have a cold, you see, and am here in my tasselled night-cap. And a long muslin gown, to boot, with a copper warming-pan at my back, and a pile of pillows.

Mary Anne is in Gloucester for the night. Visiting, I gather, one of her cousins. And will not be home until Friday. Which has put me in a very poor humour.

I miss the comforts of a hot toddy, and a solicitous manner. The pleasures of being alone wax rather thin when one is deprived of the supportive luxuries. An invalid is an ill fellow to be dependent on his own company.

So. Press on, poor Dizzy. There is much to be said, for I have not been idle since last I wrote.

I took thought, in a fit of genius, of my recent acquaintance, Inspector Goddard, and through him I have been able to trace two individuals formerly in the service of Lord Eglinton at the castle.

Both were helpful to Goddard at the time of the Tournament, I gather. One, over the affair of the gold watch, and Singlet Wilson. The other, touching another matter, of which he would say nothing.

The point is that these excellent servants, being short of cash, and without principle, have been ready to search their capacious memories for certain details about the conduct of the house guests on the morning of the Tournament.

First, Rodney Stumbleforth, a footman. For a reason that may duly emerge, I present him under the disguise of a pseudonym. A portly, pompous, officious, wholly disreputable individual, with a taste for drink, and a tendency, I gather, to have satisfied this at the expense of his late employer. Whence his enforced removal to London, and current straitened circumstances.

'The Earl of Craven's father, of course,' he recalled for me, over a stoup of porter, and a wedge of Cheddar, 'was the lover of Miss Harriette Wilson. She found him, I gather, a boring master. The son looked very splendid, I may say, in the ancestral armour. It was worn by the then Baron Hylton at the battle of Crécy. Pure Milan steel, sir, burnished blue and decorated with gold rivets. Inlaid, I believe, too, with gold, and in arabesque. He was very splendid indeed, Mr Disraeli. A proper little Knight of the Griffin. Alas and alack the day, the weight of the suit was more than he could bear, and he was forced to call for a chair in order to climb up on the back of his horse. I was privileged, I may add, to be the man chosen to bring this chair. One carved by the hand of Chippendale, sir, and normally gracing the blue saloon.'

Much more in the same vein. How the retinues of each knight were assembled in a separate room, and kept warm with coffee, and amused themselves at cards, and how each had a place to go to in the line of the procession, and the places got muddled, and the green archers of Irvine were confused with the blue Highlanders of the Knight of the Gael, and there were the beginnings of a brawl, and Eglinton himself had to clatter up in his brass armour and sort things out, and then half the servants in the castle were dressed in the wrong size of mediaeval tabard, and had to swap and go indoors again to change, and the time dragged on and on, and the clouds began to gather and gather, and the sun shrank away, and everyone in his heart of hearts knew perfectly well by one o'clock that it was going to rain.

'Imagine the crowds in the park, sir,' says the heavy Stumbleforth, gesturing with his pot of ale, and interspersing his tale with an occasional hiccup. 'I watched them coming through the long windows in the gallery, while I was clearing breakfast. There must have been a hundred thousand or more. You could see them winding through the trees in the distance like a black serpent. Women and children, soldiers and civilians, crooks and honest men. All on foot by then, since the approaches had long been blocked by a mile or more of abandoned carriages, and the railway from Irvine stopped over two miles away. Of course, the horse-drawn affair from Ardrossan came closer than this, but a claque of Campbells, they tell me, had taken over the whole train and arrived to the music of their own pipes, and in their kilts, and to the exclusion of all other sorts and conditions of men whatsoever.'

Is that how it was, Vane? Were you looking out yourself, from your tiny dressing-room in the north turret, with your lady's maid holding up your dress groaning with emeralds? Or were you still snoring, at one o'clock, and ready to dress in a last-minute splurge of haste? Well, we shall see.

Enter, my dear, my second witness. One Annie Price MacGregor. A spry, untidy, tall, ungainly redhead, with a purse of a mouth, and a pair of grey eyes like the beaks of magpies.

I met her at Bow Street, and we talked in a cell. She was in for soliciting, and will serve her time, I fear, as a common prostitute. She was caught, it would seem, *in flagrante delicto*. That is, I believe, with her back against a wall, and her skirts up, and a blackamoor from Liverpool enjoying the fruits of her best endeavours for a paltry sixpence.

This is the England, Vane, that you and your iron-masters have made. A place where a girl dismissed from service for a slovenly manner, and a fault or two in diction or memory, can find no better employment than to trail her petticoats in the gutters of Seven Dials, and mate with sailors and stevedores.

Put that idea in the furnaces of your smelting-works at Seaham Hall, and let it burn. It will burn to a fire that will scorch the walls black, and sear down, in time, the tapestries of your fine mansions, and make a mark that will never come out, and curse this Victorian age of ours for a scandal and a crime.

'I was changing linen, sir,' says Annie Price MacGregor, legs wide on a bench, and hands on her knees, while I stood with my notebook, like a constable taking a statement, and wrote down what she said. 'Several of the gentlemen was up early, sir, and I did their rooms very easy, with no one there to disturb or bother me much. But a few were late on their feet. Lying groaning there in their beds, or wrestling themselves into their suits of armour, or standing up naked as the day they was born, some of them, wanting a little bit of you-know-what in return for letting me in to make their beds. Well. I was having none of that. Not even with the Earl of Cassilis, and his pole as long as a foot ruler, I can tell you. It was more than my job was worth, it was. And then one or two. Why, they was at it already, or at it still, you know. On their silky sheets, or across their washing-tables, one or two, and I tell no lie, on the bare boards of the floor. And not all with those they ought to have been neither. Why, Lord Eglinton himself, in his own golden room, like a sort of chapel it was, all carved wooden statues of saints and babies and little painted pinnacles on the bed and those fashioned things you see in church on the ends of pews like – well, I hardly know how to say this to you, sir – like the thick stem of a man's thing with his underclothes rolled back in a frill to cover his balls. There I go. My language now! I must watch what I say. Well, who should I see peeping out there from the froth of white linen in the great unmade bed under the canopy of the wall but a certain married lady I recognised very well. And the good Lord himself, in only his bed-shirt, with his hands grasping her by the hams, and his you-know-what stuck right up her backside, and a look on her face like saying: don't stop, oh don't stop, whatever the girl may be seeing. So I closed the door, taking time only to drink it all in, and feeling as randy as a young calf in heat at the sight of what he was doing to her, and I put my basket on the floor and ran along to the slop basin and squeezed a cloth out and slid it up me and wiped what was coming out away until I felt better. And, oh, it wasn't the only time, or the only thing I saw. But I tell you straight, sir, it was one of the best, and one I can never forget until my dying day. It isn't often you see such passion. No, sir. No, indeed.'

Well, I asked her who it was, Vane. You may be sure of that. Yes, I asked her who it was, but I knew the answer already. I've known for a long time. And, of course, you know I have.

It was you, Vane. It was you with your buttocks open and your face crying for more, more, more. The way you do with me. The way you did before. The way you did when you used to say there was no one else but me.

So much for that. I feel tired. It must be the cold. Or perhaps the grey powder of Dr Sutcliffe's I am using as a specific.

Well. You are still, you say in your last letter, at Mount Stewart. Surrounded by your admiring kerns, and your ghostly bogs and your hard-hunting, hard-riding Irish squires and their horsy wives.

Charles will be in his element. I see him slapping his sides with a riding-crop, there under the Vitruvian portico, holding his finger up to see if 'twill rain.

I wonder if he did that in Ayrshire before he swung into the saddle in his armour? And if he realised why he had slept so soundly after that late flagon of Rhône wine you brought him? The one, so Annie Price MacGregor will swear, Vane, that was well and truly spiced or spiked, with a heavy sedative.

She found the box there, half-torn apart, and the label 'dangerous', in red ink, amidst the carnage of underclothes on the Aubusson carpet which the Earl of Eglinton's grandfather had specially made for his private sleeping-room.

But then you knew it was there, Vane. You put it there, tearing the powder out, and shaking it into the silver and the red wine, with your house robe flying open, and the tips of your nipples yearning for Eglinton's tawdry hands, while he lay back and fondled his piece for your amusement on the bedcovers.

And so to darkness. Darkness and a night of lonely snivelling. And my sombre thoughts of what must be written about in my letter to follow this tomorrow.

So where was I, Vane? Where was I when the rain began, and the cavalcade rolled forward through the deluge, and the Eglinton Tournament was at last under way?

Why, all done up in my morning-coat, with my best white gloves, and a plain cane, and a decent respectable tall hat, and my friend Bulwer there to hold the ring, looking up at the darkening sky on the very steps of St George's, Hanover Square, as we paid off the hansom.

'Rain, Bulwer,' say I.

'Rain, Dizzy,' says he.

And we both ducked our heads, and went in under the small side door to the vestry, as the first large drops began to patter on the stone greyhounds, and the first shopkeepers ran out of doors to draw down their shades, and pull their perishable wares indoors.

It wasn't a long service, Vane. It wasn't a grand attendance, or a great reception, afterwards. A few friends, a bottle or two of claret. A fair deal of the usual jesting and good wishes.

Then out and into the carriage, and off on the first leg of our honeymoon, with my thoughts far off and up in Ayrshire, and my last letter to you scribbled out that morning on my final occasion in my bachelor quarters at

Duke Street, and hastily sealed and handed over to a post-boy to carry to the mail and see off on its way north. By the train first, and then the steamer, and then the train again, and then the carriage, to reach your hands first thing on the following, and the Thursday, morning.

Oh yes, I thought about you. I wasn't so far gone on marriage then as I may be now. My heart, or what was left of its shattered fibres, was pinned on the sleeve of a sixteenth-century tabard, and flaunted for all to see, as I rode through the mud to my first encounter – and with whom? – in the lists.

No, there was none of that. Not for me. And not much, after all, now was there, for anyone else, either. The rain saw to that. The inevitable, unending, icy, Ayrshire, predictable rain.

'You know,' said Stumbleforth to me, with his fourth glass of ale in his fist, 'we all knew it was bound to rain. It always did. There was never a race meeting, or a private wedding, or a house party, or a stag hunt, or a fishing expedition, or even a foray out on the lawn to play croquet, sir, but that we had rain. At Eglinton Castle, rain was the universal order of the day. The young Earl knew that, sir. He grew up there. He'd been soaked to the skin a hundred times in his best clothes. And so why, I have asked myself, why, indeed, would he ever have supposed that there would be no rain for his Tournament?'

Well, I'll tell you why. I think it was pride, Vane. Sheer pride. And a sort of wilful arrogance. Not even God, in His wisdom – and for Eglinton, now, God was a hunting man, and a reasonable hard-drinking fellow, and a respecter of ladies' fine dresses, and not, as for Charlie Lamb, some monster of a guinea-pig, with a memory for imagined wrongs, and a plan to bring punishments down, oh no – not even God, so Eglinton supposed, would be so unkind. He would keep the weather fine. And would stop the rain.

Well, He didn't, Vane. I don't know why. Was it you to

blame, with your white thighs in the wrong bed, at the wrong time? I wonder. These things are noticed maybe, in Heaven. And the rain was sent down, like the flood for Noah, as a punishment for our sins.

As a punishment. Or to mime our tears, perhaps. The tears of those who care. Who have lost what they thought they had, and are forced to live on from, and forget. And have only the rain, the inclement weather, Vane, to soothe their pain.

So it rained. For whatever cause, and with no sign of relaxing its grip on Ayrshire, the rain began. At the very moment when Jane Georgiana Sheridan, lifting the skirts of her velvet and ermine dress, and shaking her raven hair, and putting on her Irish smile, and draping her cloak at her shoulders, was about to step out and be helped up on to her horse.

Lo! A single, massive drop. Then another. And another, and another, and another. And Lady Jane, wet and furious, was back in the Gothic hall, snapping her fingers, and flushing purple with rage, and using language, so Stumbleforth avers, that he never knew was current amidst the properly brought-up girls of the day.

'Not since the 1790s,' he told me, 'and the freedom of our grandmothers, and the coarser ways of the last century, have I heard such expletives, and foreign curses, and vivid English expressions of outrage and anger. No indeed. And I impassive in a powdered wig, sir, beside a bust of Charles James Fox, with my eyes front, and no sign given that I had heard one word.'

Meanwhile, as we both know, Vane, you from what you saw with your two eyes, and I from what I read in the papers, the long crocodile wound through the deluge, with Charles there in the middle under – can this really be true? – an enormous green umbrella, and the friars and the jesters and the knights themselves, and the men-at-arms and the band of the 78th Dragoon Guards, all playing for dear life in their dress uniforms, and the horses bucking and neighing, and the instruments getting waterlogged, and every now and again the whole thing grinding to a halt and everyone champing at the delay; and then on again, and the Lugton circling along beside, getting ready to overflow its inadequate banks, and the crowd rising up under makeshift rain covers and the special guests dry still but dubious under Mr Samuel Pratt's lofty wooden stands and the rain pouring off the tips of the piled lances and the pennons fluttering on the tents.

But you, of course, like the rest of the fine ladies, were still in the house. Eglinton, gallant as ever, had ridden round to suggest a closed sequence of carriages to keep you all dry. Well. You were dry enough then, maybe.

More dry than you had been in the Earl's great bath, or in his lively bed, my dear. More dry than you would be in the stands, too, as was very soon to become apparent. However.

Tea was handed round, in little fragile Sèvres cups; this detail I have from Annie Price MacGregor, who was brought downstairs, with some other chamber-maids, to hand the trays of them round, and the spicy ginger biscuits, too, and the cold little bottles of smelling-salts for those overcome by low spirits, or chills, or just in need, as many were, no doubt, of a boost for their nerves.

And at last the carriages were brought round, and the Queen of Beauty, and you, Vane, the Queen of the Tournament, and Lady Montgomerie, with her poodle and her drenched fan, and your maids-in-waiting, and your feet-warmers, and your parasols, and your coats and hats and I don't know what else to keep you amused and in fine order, all this, and all of you, were quickly carried, with the blinds down, and by a back route, to a covered entrance behind the stands. And thus conveyed secretly, and with no attention paid to your fine silks and your noble features, and your pretty ankles, into your high places.

There no one, I gather, even recognised Jane Georgiana Sheridan, even with telescopes trained from the tops of trees. There was too much mist. And according to John Richardson, as he scribbled his long despatch for *The Times* on the back of a lunch basket, and under the shelter of the dripping Press Marquee, at a distance of a hundred yards, it was only when Lady Jane's brother erected a scarlet umbrella, at the point when the roof of the stand burst, and the rain at last flowed in and down the necks and on to the bare shoulders and in between the breasts of the fine ladies there, that any of the gentlemen of the press had the slightest idea which one the Queen of Beauty might be.

By then it was four o'clock, and as yet no knight had mounted his charger and ridden down the lists. The herald, admittedly, had gone round and bawled out his announcements in a dim, low voice that no one could hear, and had been laughed at like a clown, so that when the real clown appeared, and attempted to raise some fun, he seemed positively serious in comparison, and stalked off in a fury, saying that there had been enough fooling already.

What a strange disaster it all was! Or do I exaggerate, in my pique and from my cold? You must write a reply, Vane. You must save the reputation of your noble Eglinton with a dry account of the way it truly was.

Explain, perhaps, how the common people were so good-humoured, and raised a cheer for his energy and his great concern when he rode round in his golden suit and was so polite and apologetic to everyone. The perfect sportsman to whom the English – and even the Scottish, so it would seem – are always inclined to warm.

Elaborate, perhaps, on the way that the rain has been overemphasised. How it only started at three o'clock, how it slackened a little by six, how there were several courses, in time, and a sword fight, and a proper competition held with the points recorded in due form by the judges on their tallies.

Outline, from your personal experience, how the ladies bore their misfortunes with candour, and with integrity, and with, on the whole, much less of the swearing and talking like fishwives than my doubtless biased informant has led me to believe.

Assure me that neither the dauntless virgins, like Lady Louisa, nor the serene matrons, as Lady Jane may have been, were known to have even heard of, far less been heard to mutter, such coarse expressions as ... Well, I blush to write out the words.

Write, though. And be the witness to what was done, Vane. And forgive, now I know you will, my commentary on your own behaviour. 'Tis all in the past, as Lyndhurst used to say, when his new mistresses would upbraid his history.

Of course. And we love each other now. Of course we do. And Eglinton is the prey of a heartless harridan, for his sins. God rest his fornicating soul.

YOUR ENORMOUS LETTER – I have just re-counted the pages, and arrive, still, at the formidable tally of seventeen – has been languishing, although not, I may say, unread or unpondered upon, at the back of my file of unanswered correspondence.

Languishing, I fear, for far too long. I can plead only one cause – a real sense that your points were all well taken. I have gone too far.

Yes, Vane, I know I have. But then so did you. Let us make a truce on that, and begin again. I will spare you my own seventeen sheets of reiterated, and no doubt boring, squabble.

Instead, let me praise yours. I picture you there day after day, pacing with your wolfhounds across the bogs and the moorland, surrendering the reins or the leashes to Sean or Megeen or O'Connell or Miss Raferty or whichever other of your local servants accompanies your solitary walks, and licking your pencil for a few further condemnatory and trenchant sentences.

They certainly flow, Vane. You have never before written with such dash and force. You should take up novel-writing yourself. The Brontës would have to look to their laurels. And as for Miss Ferrier, you could swear her into a cocked hat. I am quite certain of that.

You are right, of course. My remarks about Eglinton, while undoubtedly couched in the best of English, were presented in the worst of taste. And were libellous, too, you say.

Well, I wonder now. The courts are a funny world. One remembers the odd affair of Melbourne and Caroline Norton. What party derived much satisfaction from all of that? Not one, I say.

Nor would Eglinton, as you very well know, my dear, be much mollified by a course or two with pointed lances at the Old Bailey. Truth will not be mocked. And nor, I fancy, will the good Earl's jealous wife.

A truce, I say. You are full of emphasis on the sturdy question of Charles's manhood, and his vigorous pursuit of his conjugal rights out there amongst the potatoes – if there are any left – and the horse fairs.

One page on that subject might really have sufficed. I don't suppose that either of us have ever doubted the ability of your stalwart Lord to get up a fine head of steam – as it were – on the right occasion. But the autobiography of the stoker, complete with details of the number of shovelfuls of coal required to heat the boiler, is not necessarily the only way to underline the power of an old locomotive.

I agree. He was ever a noble stud. This has not always, however, prevented his bed-mate from elaborating her portfolio elsewhere. To mingle my metaphors.

Now has it, Vane? So let me hear no more of these copulations among fishing-baskets, and couplings to the halloo of the hunting-horn. I can use my imagination. Thank you.

Apart from your own letter, I may say, I have a splendid and lengthy epistle to answer from a Mr Nathaniel Parker Willis. The author, as I am sure you will recall, of *Loiterings of Travel*.

No? Well, I must confess that this eminent work of

literature was one that I, too, had failed to encounter. It is, I should add, available directly from the author, who has printed it at his own expense, and in florid lavender boards, for a mere two dollars and fifty cents.

You should read it, Vane. Mr Willis is a man of parts, and a man of perception. His account of your dress at the Tournament – 'a divine confection of contrasting velvets' – is only one of many delights in his book.

I was given the name, of course, by my ever-valuable connection, Inspector Goddard. It turns out that he was able to assist Mr Willis in Ayrshire over the little matter of a quarrel in a pot-house.

In return, our American cousin sent him this gilded memento of his travels in Europe, and a covering letter reminding him of his assistance in warding off the assault and battery of a drunken gaggle of Scottish steel-workers.

So off to Willis I wrote. Hoping, and not without reason, as it turns out, that he would favour me with a more detailed survey of that far-off rain-flooded Wednesday than he had been able to commit to print.

I have his ruled foolscap, and his blackberry copperplate, here in my hand. A notable writer, with more than a touch of the orotund. Apart from his tale of the great struggle between Eglinton and Waterford, and the mass retreat through the rain, to which I shall return, he is full of useful opinions, and occasional scraps of information, on the future of our American trade.

'You mark my words, Mr Disraeli, sir,' he writes, 'in twenty years' time from this day, I predict that the United Kingdom of Great Britain will be importing half of her meat, and three-quarters of her grain, from the great farms of the Midwest. It requires only the means of transportation – and the steamship has given us that – to see salt pork and Iowa wheat in every market of your country. And at knock-down prices!'

He may well be right, Vane. The negroes, I hear, are

picking cotton for no more than food and shelter, and the poor whites in the north earn less than a penny a day, some say, for packing meat and cutting maize. We can never compete with that.

I thank the Lord that no one has yet found a way of storing the carcass of a lamb in cubes of ice, as the Swiss, they say, preserve their corpses in winter before their burial. But it may yet come. It may yet come.

In the meanwhile, Mr Nathaniel Parker Willis, owner of a canning company in South Bend, Indiana, is my authority for declaring that the American economy is fast overtaking our own, and that the Corn Laws, in time, will be our only protection.

What use will your cheap iron and your seam coal be then, Vane? When the price of a loaf is dictated by the wage of a Red Indian in St Louis, and the price of a ton of coke by the miners of Pittsburgh, you may shut up shop and go home to your winter gardens at Wynyard, and let Seaham colliery close down, and your grimy face-workers apply to emigrate.

Here is Nathaniel Parker Willis, a fine swaggering fellow with dark sideburns, and a gold watch on a chain, to judge from the daguerreotype he encloses, and he and his like are going to rule the industrial world. The Yankee magnates, Vane. The new gods of the Capitalist world.

I sense the sort of energy we are dealing with from this account of the excellent Willis's visit to Ayrshire. How he was able to commandeer a seat in a first-class cabin on the *Royal Sovereign*, in return for a brace of Havana cigars. How he won ninety dollars – or twenty-five pounds, I suppose – in a game of poker with some of the swell-mob. And how he held on to his winnings by flourishing a pearl-handled pistol under the nose of Little Cricket Jim himself.

How he rode up to Irvine in the steam train with a friend of Liz Howard's and how he found all the rooms at the

Eglinton Arms booked up and so strode upstairs and opened the first door he saw and raised his tall hat and had his jacket and shirt off and washed the sweat from his body at a hand-basin while two chamber-maids and a woman in stockings and a towel behind a screen screamed blue murder and thought he had come to steal their virginity or their lives or probably both.

And then how he laid down a crackling fiver – his only English banknote – and thanked them all from the bottom of his heart and buttoned his shirt up and went downstairs and strode out again into the street and found a bed and a sound supper and a contentious night's conversation with the local Presbyterian minister.

Mr Willis, it seems, is a man of great resource. He was able, on the morning of the Tournament, to be at the castle early, and walk straight in through the front door into the hall, and go to and fro examining the last-minute preparations like a head carpenter or a Duke's valet.

'Why, I saw the Knight Marshall', says he, 'hitch up his trousers and shove a half-bottle of Scotch whisky down his waistband and hawk up a stream of blue phlegm in a spittoon shaped like a brass tortoise. I saw Lady Jane Georgiana Sheridan, the Queen of Beauty, all got up in her ermine dress and scratching under the armpits like a chimpanzee with the jiggers. I saw Lord Waterford in the top half of his armour squatting on a porcelain jerry-can with his face contorted like a walnut in a pickling jar. Why, Mr Disraeli, you ask for the soft underbelly, to put it in my own words, of what was everywhere going on. Well, sir, I can tell you.

'I never did ever see such magnificence or such God-awful squalor. Fine ladies and gentlemen sweltering in tight clothes that never did fit them, and needing to answer the many needs of nature, sir, without a proper button or loop to release and find an easement.

'Still, I will say this. When I got me down to the stands,

and lit up my last cigar, and saw Lord Eglinton canter down the lists on his bay stallion, and Lord Waterford run up the other side on his white mare, and the trumpets flashing in the rain, and the two of them rushing along that high fence as if they was going to kill each other stone dead, and when I heard the lances break, snap, in two, and saw Lord Eglinton rein up and throw away the broken piece and then ride on and round, and Waterford bow his head and raise his hand, I will say this was all a very notable and moving exhibition, sir, and I ain't seen any rodeo, not through the whole of Texas or the Western territories, that was anything like the equal of it for spectacle and glamour. No, sirree.

'You English have a way of doing these things, Mr Disraeli. There was a kinda cool, devil-may-care sort of way that Lord Eglinton rode around. Why, we just, well, we don't have that in Arizona.'

So there you are, Vane. A testimonial to our dear William from the other side of the Atlantic. And one supported by many another passage in Mr Willis's hectic foolscap.

I am writing this, by the way, standing up. You would hardly guess how pleasant it comes to be. I have been suffering from a sore place – a mild abscess, I believe – in the tender part of my forks. The sort of thing, of course, one hardly dares to mention at Crockford's.

But the irritation has almost gone, I find, from this new habit of writing on my feet. I completed the first part of this letter at a window-sill in a corridor of the House of Commons. The last few pages have been accomplished in my dressing-room, at a small Wellington chest, in an alcove.

Three cheers, I say, for the great Duke, for inventing – as they say he did in the Peninsula – this most useful form of tall cabinet, at which one may labour in writing without the need to bend one's back.

Let me give you, however, some gems from Mr Willis's grim account of the great retreat. You may not be aware of the full horror of that squelching journey, when over a hundred thousand, like the troops of Napoleon retiring from Moscow through the snow, had to drag their soaking way home, to Irvine, to Ardrossan and beyond.

You were safely back in the castle, Vane. Stripping off your dripping coronet with the help of a sympathetic maid, and a glass of Russian tea. Warming your portly buttocks before a blazing fire. And with a good dinner, and a night's melancholy jesting and analysis to look forward to.

Not so Nathaniel Parker Willis. Who spent a weary six hours in rain and darkness helping women and children to flounder through the marshy grounds to the railway. Not so, for that matter, one Sarah Wildman McConnichie, who died in the early hours of the following morning, resting her head on her father's arms under a hawthorn bush, with her bedraggled legs in a muddy ditch. About whom the medical report, made out later in the Glasgow General Hospital, recorded 'exposure' as the precipitating cause of her death by asthma.

Not so those who had no carriages, or whose carriages, or waggons, or broughams, or flies, just stuck in a quagmire, and were abandoned until the following day. Not so all those who trailed or waded or were carried or helped through the great sea of solid, unending Scottish mud that the overflowing Lugton had rendered the fine purlieus of Eglinton Castle.

Not so those whose expensive clothes were ruined by the leaking roof of Samuel Pratt's cheaply run-up stand, where the tiles failed to overlap, and so let water trickle through. Not so, even more, those who stood all day in the downpour, and then set out for home without knowing what they had seen, since they were too far off to hear the names of the knights mumbled into the wind by the herald, and thus marched or shambled, in one great grey and scaly-backed or umbrella-surfaced crocodile, groaning and spitting and swearing and jostling and kneeing and kicking each other, in the worst of tempers, and the poorest of spirits, back to their unheated hovels, and their fireless manses, and their flea-ridden hotels, and their cramped lodgings, all over Ayrshire for a radius of twenty miles or more.

But then you were in your bath, Vane. You were washing your fleshy shoulders with a loofah. You were pouring scented lotions into the tub to make the water smooth for your skin. Water, yes. But for you it was lovely stuff, dear Vane.

It was warm and solacing. It was under control. It was what the rich can use to dissolve away the dirt and clamour of the day. A humble servant, Vane. A sweet and caressing mistress.

But not for the poor. Not for the ordinary unaided masses out there in the pelting, windy cold. Imagine them, my darling. Think about them for once, if you can. That night, and however many more.

YES, VANE, I KNOW it was not a success. Your hurried message – very nearly illegible, my dear – told me nothing new. It was quite apparent when we parted, I may say, that matters had not evolved as they might.

I am sorry to hear of your soreness. No doubt the breezes of Killarney, and the loving attentions of the gallant and familiar Charles, will soon restore you to good health and sound physique.

I warn you, though. These mild lesions do tend in their development in the direction of a greater irritation before they mend. At least, that has been the case with mine.

First, an aching sensation at the top of the leg. Hmmm. You have had that? Well. It sounds the same. Second, a redness, a diffused flush of the skin, followed by a massive swelling.

No, you say. But then, perhaps the symptoms of the ailment are different in a woman. You mention your leg, but I am guessing that you are perhaps being modest, or reticent.

I suspect, Vane, your genitalia. There. A vulgar Latin word for a French and frivolous piece of machinery. On the lips, to be blunt, my dear, it may hardly enlarge as it can on the noble foreskin.

So that really you do, I fear, suffer from the same malaise as I have done. Is it in the air? Or does it work – alas – by the contagion of the anxious flesh? That is, by fornication.

Well. The whore of Babylon might have known the answer. For I fear this complaint – to judge from the information I have derived through discreet enquiry amongst some friends – is not unknown, or unheard-of, in the annals of medical science, or the private journals of the great lovers.

Castiglione, they say, has his commentary. Casanova makes an oblique mention. Lady Belle Sejourné is believed to have contracted the malady from an improper congress with her Boston terrier.

Still, to the third symptom. You must watch out for the blisters. The pustules, dare I call them? And then the breaking down of the tissues, and the raw scar.

Ugh. I have endured the cycle, and I warn you to be ready. The last of the states, in its way, may seem the worst, and impede the easy movement of the limbs.

But fear not. The thing goes, and one feels entirely oneself again. Although not – as you will have gathered from our experience in the rose arbour – until the expiry of some weeks, and the completion of the pustule stage.

I attempted to have you, Vane, with a flaming blister on the end of my organ. Now you know the facts. I was not unable, or *impuissant*, or whatever else you want to call it. I was simply in pain.

So that when I bent you over the rustic sill, and hustled up your voluminous petticoats – obligingly, yes, I do grant you this – most obligingly cut away and made free from any encumbrance at your forks, and when I stood forward, and, opening my trousers, reaching out my hand as though to pluck a tea rose over your bare shoulder, plunged, or aimed to plunge, my now vibrant member into your, alas, a little unready, and rather primly dry and resistant orifice, I felt a savage and lacerating disinclination to proceed. A sensation, I may say, as of a carrot-grater scoring the skin off the end of my penis.

I am coarse. Yes, but exact, my dear. You were wrong. I was not unloving, neither do I find your body, or the thought of it, unappetising. I am still your slave. At least in the physical sense.

But, Vane, I am weary. Coquetry is one thing, but withdrawal is very much another. Here was I, feeling quite restored to my normal vigour, and eager for a fresh encounter with the straits of my inconvenience, the Scylla and Charybdis, as it were, the rocks and the whirlpool, of your little flickering lower tongue and your tingling honey-pot, restored and eager, I say, and with a folio of engravings to show you, and a whole afternoon to spare for the exercise. And what happens? I reach your door, I knock, as I am wont, and raise my hand, and I am handed a folded sheet of paper on a wooden tray, and informed that her Ladyship has returned for the season to Ireland.

Surely this is hardly the way to treat an old friend? You might easily have laid bare your plans when we walked amongst the cherry trees, or lingered over our cup of chocolate in the salon. But no. You gave me every reason to suppose that you would remain in town until Sunday. And that we should meet again this afternoon.

I am pacing my study, Vane. I am most upset. I am angry, too. And bored. I go to and fro between my little groups of columns, and pick at the volumes of blue books, and unseat an encyclopaedia, or a copy of the *Athenaeum*, and spin the pages and feel listless, and am – really am – unendurably out of sorts.

I shall pause, in fact, and continue later. A course of what George Smythe would call the Egyptian badminton may work off a little of my surplus energy. You may think on this, my dear, and of what is thus wasted.

Do you know the name of Octavius Hill? I hardly thought

that you would. And yet the admirable Octavius is already, I understand, at the head of his admittedly somewhat farouche, not to say unheard-of, profession.

Octavius Hill, you see, is a professional of the camera obscura. He has a small studio in Earnley Place, complete with golden velvet curtaining, and a suite of balloon-back chairs in the best of taste, and a very distinguished *madame* in a black veil and a cameo brooch to receive his clients.

I know. It sounds very much like a Naples bordello. And perhaps it is, on those careful occasions when he prepares, with the help of a willing model, what are now described as life studies, that is, my dear, oleograph prints of women in a state of nature.

These were not, however, what the voluble and elusive Octavius treated me to an exhibition of – more is the pity – when I visited him this morning on my way to the House.

You see, he was up in Ayrshire. On holiday, as I understand, with the family of his intended wife, a wench from Prestonpans, with green ear-rings, and a flair for making treacle scones, with which she regaled me, as I sat near Octavius on his working sofa and leafed through the fruits of his Scottish tour.

'Oh yes, yes, indeed,' he said – he says everything twice over, to give it emphasis, it would seem – 'we were over in Galloway, in Galloway, yes, and we heard, Marie and I, we heard of the Tournament, and we felt, well, we knew of course, that we really had to go over, I mean to hire a coach, which we did, you know, hire a coach and ride over to Eglinton Castle, and yes, yes I did take my camera, and my plates, and we hired things to wear, yes, fifteenth-century clothes we hired, and look, these are the ones.'

And while he went on and on like this, and I chewed my scones, and grinned away at the irrepressible Marie, who kept smoothing down the watered silk at her waist, and making me wonder who it might be who did the modelling for the life studies, out there came one after another, from a great vellum-bound box, a series of truly magnificent large yellowy-green photographic prints, very like engravings, or rather like mezzotints, with a splendid muzzy shadow effect, and a quite remarkable sense of being faithful to the lineaments of the people they were reproducing.

'Why,' I said, 'Mr Hill,' and I meant every word of this, dear Vane, I tell you, 'these are a most impressive record of what you saw. I would very willingly do a sitting myself some day, if that would be possible, to arrange an appropriate "taking", or what you may call it, of my features and clothing.'

And so I shall, Vane, so I shall. I am down already in the active Octavius's little black book of appointments, and will duly present myself, complete with Mary Anne for a partner, on the 19th of August next.

Then to be seated, or stood by a suitable plinth, and caught in profile or full face, Mary Anne in her best purple at my side – although it will come out, of course, in black and white, or rather, this dim, rather eloquent sepia shade – and thus to be studied from under a dark serge cloth by a sort of humped monster with one arm forward to squeeze a leather bulb, and cause a flash of light, and so enshrine my image on the treated plate for posterity. A splendid thought, Vane. A splendid thought.

Imagine if I could engage you to pose naked yourself – well, incognito, of course – for the excellent Octavius who is, of course, as passion-free as a doctor or an undertaker in his work, and thus obtain a full folio record of your sprawling body, front and rear, with nothing, perhaps, but a flourish or two of gauze or scarfing to grant the pictures a flavour of decency!

It beats etching, Vane. And is fast and faithful. No hours of lying still on an itchy mattress while some voluptuous Greek or Italian sweeps his fertile brushes across a stretched canvas, and fillets your nakedness of every crack and cranny of its privacies.

No more of that. A mere ten or fifteen minutes at most, warmed by the thoughtful provision of an oil heater near the divan, and then back, and behind a screen, and the thing is all done, and most tastefully, too, and for no more than the price of Cotman's Beauties of Norfolk.

It will cause a revolution in the world of art, Vane. You mark my words. Why, you should see what Octavius has put on plate already. His studies of Eglinton Castle, and many of the scenes at the Tournament, are a record to rival the best of Doyle or Cobbold.

It was Stumbleforth who told me about the stick fights on the morning after the rain, and how Charlie Lamb and Louis Napoleon, among others, to alleviate their boredom, came to blows with brooms and mop handles in the derelict and rain-sodden marquee.

I asked Octavius Hill about this, and it turns out that he was admitted on the Thursday morning and did, in fact, make several studies of this very event. You should see the likenesses.

Why, Eglinton has come out in one with his hand on his hip like a bone-setter's model of a human body in rags and basketwork. The original thin man to the life.

There are several, too, of the combatants in their morning-clothes, with their cigars lit, and their mops truculently held like proper swords and lances, and all the servants in the front row gawping and staring with their mouths open, and one or two with their heads turned the wrong way, or their hands moving and blurring like birds flying.

That happens, you see, if you don't sit still. It seems that the lens, or the camera eye, as it were, has to sort of blink, rather slowly, like a barn owl, and then stay open for a long time during which it records whatever is going on. So that something that moves is taken as moving, and thus vague, and unclear.

I am quite, you see, the accomplished man of the camera.

And may even set up as an amateur myself, and make studies of my friends. Beware, my dear. I may track you down in Mount Stewart, and forge a lasting impression of the lusty Charles in the very act.

What an alluring blur that would make! I wonder whether the presence of the camera would impede the progress of the earnest seeker after pleasure. An interesting speculation.

At any rate, it had no effect on the vigour of the stick-fighters, to judge from the studies. There we have Charlie Lamb, in breeches and open-neck shirt, evidently laying on like a real swordsman across Louis Napoleon's back.

'Which was not, sir,' says Stumbleforth, 'an entirely satisfactory state of affairs. There was bad blood between those two young gentlemen. As all could see.'

Now I wonder why, Vane? Was it Liz Howard who was giving the trouble? Our Charlie, we all know, is a very susceptible young fellow, and he may, I doubt it not, have been casting his eyes a little further than the delectable thighs of his entertaining Charlotte.

Who was by then, of course, back safe in her little hotel room, playing patience, and waiting without patience for the closed brougham to return and whisk her to a second assignation in the Eglinton woods.

But, well, who knows? Was Charlie eager to draw comparisons? Had his days on the roof of the Eyre Arms given him a taste for the presumptuous cleavage of an older woman's bosom? In a word, Liz Howard's?

That would hardly have pleased Prince Louis, now would it? Well. It might account for his black scowl in the oleographs, and his broom striking, clearly with a lot of force and venom, across poor Charlie's unprotected knee. Or so it seems.

It might account, this too – and this I have kept until last, dear Vane – for the smirk of amused enjoyment on your own florid features, as you loll there on a bench, and fan yourself, and are evidently delighted that William Eglinton is no longer attracted (and indeed why should he be, with your own sumptuous hams at his side?) by the whore's tricks, and the subtle fingers, of the tart he once called – and I have the authority of Annie Price MacGregor on this, who was cleaning the slops bucket, and overheard him talking to Waterford – 'the most accomplished and abandoned fornicatress with whom it has ever been my privilege to engage'.

I must end, Vane. The western post is due to leave in an hour. I shall write again.

YOU HAVE MISSED very little in the fête at Gunnersbury. Not, of course, that you would have come, my dear. Nor been invited, for that matter. The Rothschilds, I gather, have always thought you rather arrogant. Well, it takes one to know one.

Madame mère is quite the battleaxe. Must be eighty now, if she is a day, and looks every inch of her years. She moves in a sort of wheeled frame, like a child learning to walk, and one has to watch one's feet.

Indeed, I have nearly lost the use of my ankle bone, through her edging ever closer – with ear-trumpet, I may say, outstretched – in an attempt to absorb my shouted witticisms. The wheels ground very close.

But for the providential yelping of a small hairless dog – one of those Mexican toys – and the sharp eyes of a young footman, I might be in hospital for my pains. With my pains and for my pains, as it were.

As it is, I have made my excuses, dodged old Skimbleshanks with his bad breath and his foul stories, and found myself a lonely corner to the rear of the refreshment pavilion.

Here, balancing my French ice and my English turkey slices on a bamboo table, I am taking stock of the weather –

which bids fair to rain at any moment – and improving the still-shining and now quieter hour by the penning of a few more lines to my absent friend.

Well. I hope I may still call you that. The drying out of the scars, I may say, has made it easier to sit in comfort, and I hope, in all charity, that you are fast approaching the same condition.

I am scarcely in the mood for parties, and this one seems unusually full of rattles, place-seekers, and plain bores. We go to and fro, from temple to arbour, and from terrace to fountain, chatting, chatting, chatting, and all in the dull marble vein of so many garden statues.

I feel I could engage in a more rewarding conversation with the pouting cupid at my shoulder than with sad Lord this or fat Lady that or little Sir silly Willy the other. The Rothschilds do try very hard, but the chosen people are awfully prone to be saturnine and practical.

What wouldn't I give for a bright pair of Irish eyes, or thighs, or a little touch of your spry Mount Stewart sickness! London, dear Vane, is in the doldrums. The sores and the horsy squires may oppress, but the flatness of Rothschild wit has fewer bubbles than American champagne.

It has cast, I fear, its own glacial hues over the current mood in my mind.

I feel, however, very much in the position of the Scots Lord in the play. I am so far advanced, 'twere as tedious to return as go o'er. And yet the accumulating memoirs on my desk at Grosvenor Gate are becoming as thick and incapacitating as Macbeth's own sea of blood.

For example. I have a portly ledger, bound in half-morocco, with fine endpapers, and a gilt superscription, enshrining the personal recollections of one Dr Guthrie, of Airdrie, now retired.

The excellent leech, then a mere stripling of sixty-seven, was employed by Eglinton, I gather, as his field surgeon.

Arriving in frock-coat, and with brass-clasped bag at the ready, he sat under a special silken awning of his own, at the brink of the arena, and took his fair share of mud-splashing on the Wednesday, and then, in due course, of sawdust-sprinkling on the Friday.

The ledger comes to life at the moment when the Knight of the Swan was wounded in the wrist, thrown from his horse, and borne, bleeding profusely, to the fence around the lists.

Jerningham, yes. Do you remember, Vane? I gather that our awkward Norfolk knight was once again the star performer of this final joust. Managing, alas, to be cut to the bone by a round-headed wooden lance. A rare achievement.

'A splinter of some five inches in length,' records the dry doctor, and I imagine him kneeling there by the recumbent knight like a mourner on a tomb, 'piercing the skin a little above the heel-bone of the thumb, and entering the main artery in the left forearm, there severing the tissue and causing a copious flux of blood, remained lodged in the patient's arm, and required a careful extraction, using a number three scalpel bathed in alcohol, and being drawn slowly, and I fear somewhat to the patient's discomfort, so as to avoid any risk of the wood snapping and a portion remaining inside, and thus corrupting and poisoning the arm. The operation was conducted in five minutes, with the sun shining, and my boy spreading his coat to keep the dazzle out of my eyes, a surprising necessity after the pronounced deluge of the previous day's jousting. The patient remained conscious, his teeth gritted, and his eyes closed, and upon the completion of the extraction called for a bottle of whisky, which he proceeded to swallow in large gulps, and then pour in a generous douche over the wound. It may have helped staunch the blood, I know not. However, there was shortly some sign of clotting, and I bound up the arm in a two-inch cotton bandage, and the man rose to his feet, swayed and fainted. Shortly, fortunately, he was again revived with the whisky, shook his head, and was carried by his squire, and a local farmer, into his tent, where I believe he rested for an hour and was then quite recovered. The mercies of God are considerable. Thank Heaven for our medical skills, and that I was able to save the poor fellow's arm, and maybe his life.'

Why, I have letters from those who catered, and lists of guests from the estate manager, and extracts from their diaries from the wives and daughter of Highland advocates, and the hotel and steamer bills of a deceased clergyman from Ludlow, in Shropshire, and a copy of the deposition sworn against Elephant Smith by an Irvine hotel-keeper for refusing to pay a bill, and the notes made by Maclise for his drawings, and the recollections written down by Landseer, after a streaming cold, and more or less incomprehensible, when he had stood in the deluge for seven hours perfecting his sketch of a Scotch wolfhound in the train of the Knight of the Gael; I have all these, and photographic images, and pieces cut from newspapers, and Doyle's book, and three or four others, and my own now very copious records of talk and abuse and praise and blame; all these, I say, and last of all, and frayed away now almost to a thin Japanese gauze, my dear, your own single-sheet letter written in reply to my own from Duke Street on the morning of my wedding, my own many pages, torn from my heart's valves, and imbued with more emotion than I can now recall, and informing you, of what you must surely long since by then have heard, and have guessed, and have understood – the reasons for my marriage.

I have your own letter by heart, Vane. And a brutal, callous severance of a close and loving relationship it makes, in very truth.

'Adieu,' you wrote. Adieu, indeed. 'You should hear again' – and indeed I should have heard again, and often, if there were any faith or love in female hearts – 'before I leave England. But I would not delay writing one line to assure you of the interest I take' – the interest, forsooth – 'in your happiness. Which I hope is now fixed.'

Aye, fixed, then, as you well know. And not with Mary Anne, you witch. 'Believe me yours.' And I did, Vane, I did. 'Very truly.' Yes, very very truly. 'F.A. Vane Londonderry.' F.A., indeed. And Londonderry, Vane. As though to a tradesman, or a groom asking for a reference.

I say no more. I tore it open at the window of our little honeymoon hotel in Tunbridge Wells, as you knew I would, and it made the tears gleam in my eyes. For rage, and for pain.

It was the last letter I had for three years and the last, I think, that you wrote, and with a cold, calculating completeness, before you left Ayrshire and Eglinton, and took ship with Charles for Liverpool and then for Austria, and for your extensive travels in Russia, and in the Middle East.

What lovers were there, Vane? What swollen Arabs, or dusky Moors, to equal the bony passion of your Ayrshire Earl, or your Duke Street Israelite? I wonder.

Oh yes, you have told me. Many times. You made a triumphal progress to match the cavalcades of your dear Frederick amongst the bedouin. And with more to show for it, in costly jewels, and Moorish rugs, and the dark memories of your nights of sin.

Poor Charles! I pity him there, with his ageing complaisance, and his anxiety to keep his own barque moored, as it were, at the quay of passion, your bare hip, and your bared groin.

Hard things to miss, Vane. Hard things to lose. And in truth, perhaps, not always lost. Or not for long. And not for always. No, not for always.

Charles with his brusque member, and his ham-fisted manners, and his anxious, frowning attentiveness, yes, Charles is back in the saddle again, as you have too firmly insisted. I, too, no doubt. In my time.

In my time, Vane. And Eglinton, my love? I wonder. Has

William shaken off the toils of that excellent and insipid virago, and had his further helping, his eager and second go at the dumpling, delving in where he did before?

Has he, Vane? Have you had him again? Have you taken Eglinton back, as you took back me? And not only Eglinton. What others have gone and come? I wonder now. Has Waterford? Or Jerningham?

I see you there at the banquet, magnificent amidst the flagons of malmsey, and the quarts of hippocras, and the pots of swan, and the lamprey pies, and the primrose tarts, and the eight hundred pounds of prime turtle, escorted from London by a hired chef on the steamer *Sir William Wallace*. Eating, Vane. Eating and being eaten. Drinking, and being drunk. The witch of Endor in the cave of plenty.

Yes, you were quite the most dazzling of all the women there in your pounds of emeralds, your glittering surcoat of special green, your encrusted surface of faceted, icy jewels. More desirable than Aunt Jane in her dahlia satin; than Lady Montgomerie in her tasteful cerise; than Lady Graham with that string of pearls around her waist like a skipping, or perhaps like a whipping, rope; than Mrs Campbell, trimmed, as they say, with bullion; than the Duchess of Montrose in her diamond stomacher; than little Louisa Stuart in her transparent muslin, like a dragonfly on heat; than Liz Howard – no, surely Liz Howard was kept away in only her oil and her powder, and Charlie's Charlotte, too, with her hair down to the back of her knees; then, yes, to be sure, more desirable even than the Queen of Beauty herself, splendid in ermine at the right hand of your panting paramour, the Lord of the Tournament.

You were wanted, Vane. For sure. But were you had? And by whom? By whom, Vane? By the thirteen knights, one after another, with the other women watching and envious, on the gilded, rose-embroidered throne in the ballroom, while the candles guttered in their blistering sockets, and the footmen licked their lips, and shifted in their tight breeches, and your husband snored his wine off with his head in a bucket in the pouring-room, and Eglinton, too, after taking his turn, replete, and unsatisfied, went away and had the remainder out along the spine of Louisa Stuart, or of Jane Georgiana Sheridan, or of who knows what anonymous, desperate serving-wench, squeaking like a little stuck pig on a wooden stool at the back of the scullery?

You will write, I hope, and upbraid my overheated imagination. You will tell me that I have coarsened a noble occasion, and trailed its glories in the mire.

Of course. But I am jealous by turns, Vane. And jealous men see life in lurid colours.

THE SESSION IS OVER, and once again we are packing to travel. It is almost, I realise, a year since the letter I wrote en route for Paris drew your fire, as it were, and renewed our acquaintance.

The loops and turns of these last months have been more than convoluted, and I am eager for a rest. The glades and galleries of the Deepdene, and the soothing banalities of Hope's conversation, will no doubt supply me with all I need.

We are bidden for a month, and may stay as long. I know not. There are straws in the wind, hints of new alliances, talk of a party newspaper.

Leisure to write, however, will be more than welcome. And warm fires, and good claret, and a proper stock of writing-paper. One grows used to the spongy tissues of the aristocracy, and the powdery ink they serve.

Not so Hope. He is a miracle of attentiveness. Asking already how many quires of my cream-laid vellum to have pressed and prepared. And what sorts of ink I shall want to use, whether blues or purples, or a choice of the two.

'And pens, Dizzy,' says he, in his last letter. 'Will you bring your own, or shall I order a stock of my own favourite Hungarian quills? Whatever you prefer.'

The man is a jewel. A boring jewel, perhaps, like a valuable and outmoded family heirloom, but a jewel. But, yes. I shall take my own pens – I am cutting one now – and I shall stick to the wings of the British geese that have so far always served me well.

Fiction is in the air, and the public is ready to read, and thus to listen. I may change the mind of England by the pressure of the pen rather sooner, I suspect, than by the process of Parliament.

Hmmm. I am growing too alliterative. I must be careful. Yesterday was the anniversary of our wedding, and I have been following my practice during the last three years of improving the occasion by addressing Mary Anne in verse.

Don't worry. I have no intention of inciting a former mistress – or a future one, for that matter – by an extensive quotation from my *rimes d'occasion*. You will know the sort of thing I contrive.

There were few candles, of course, for the recitation, and no company. We dined alone in the mauve sewing-room – well, it isn't really mauve, but it always seems to be by candlelight – and I unburdened myself of my nine short stanzas.

Clapping hands, and a kiss. Mary Anne is ever appreciative. And then up to bed, with a glass apiece of orange curaçao, and a few gay steps of a country dance, and so into the feathers, and close to the warming-pan.

A life, dear Vane. A dull but secure and comfortable existence, for sure. Less diversified, and less active and ambitious, no doubt, than your own continually energetic arrangements with the lugubrious Charles. But then you are quick to stress how exceptional he is.

I am writing this, by the by, in my dressing-room. I have a fine view through the door – as in one of those Dutch pictures which always tend to make things look more mysterious – of Mary Anne with her stays loose, and the maid smoothing the whalebone over her hips.

Distance, no doubt, lends an enchantment. Strange, though, how I never see my wife so clearly as an object of affection or desire as when we are about to leave home. The litter of trunks, and the general air of disruption, make the familiar seem a trifle, as it were, naughty.

This is doubtless why young couples are always dismissed, as soon as possible after their marriages, on a lengthy honeymoon. The turning carriage wheels, and the revolutions of hotel bedrooms, prevent the onset, at least for some weeks, of any sense of marital ennui.

So it was with us, Vane. In spite of the awful rain, and the absence of a proper umbrella, our early days in Tunbridge Wells passed in a mild euphoria. I can still recall with a measure of tenderness the peeling shutters of our dilapidated little hotel in the Pantiles.

Which is really saying something. When one considers my state of mind. After the fourth day, indeed, when the downpour slackened, and I took a turn by myself to buy supplies of tobacco, thoughts of the house guests at Eglinton Castle, and the rusting armour, and the praise and the solicitation of our disappointed William were still very prominent in my mind.

You had left, of course, the two of you, Charles in his uniform and his cocked hat, like the grand personage he felt he was, and that Eglinton thought him, too, and you in your cloak and your amethysts, with a flow of servants to hand you your carrying baggage, and a flood of remaining nobility to wave your victoria on its way.

Stumbleforth has recalled for me the flash of your ankle, with a little silver chain round it, he says, like a French cocotte, as you were handed up to your seat, and arranged your ample skirts. You must have set the fashion for those, that year.

Scandal stood by with her lips closed, and Honour wept for pity. Poor Eglinton! He had little more to look forward to than a pair of scathing letters, and perhaps a scented garter, from St Petersburg, or maybe from Istanbul.

It was more than he deserved. Your thoughts were already ahead of your dipping horses, and your skimming prow, far out in the luxurious East, on the plains of Russia, and the cushions of the Levant.

Of course, there was a dinner, weeks later, and the men all raised their glasses to Eglinton in the hotel at Irvine, and solaced his regrets with pork fillets, and haggis, and the best malts from the glens. But then that was to thank him for his Tournament, not to console him for the loss of his mistress.

Charles was absent on that occasion, though present, I think, in spirit. He must have been kept busy, on your travels, with his correspondence about the Eglinton Memorial, if I am to believe the account supplied by Jerningham concerning the quarrelling on the committee.

You will not yet, I fancy, have seen the finished sculpture. I understand from Maclise, who has enjoyed a preview, that there is to be an official unveiling, and a presentation, later this year.

Eight feet high, I gather, including its wooden base, and enclosed in glass, like a heap of iced buns in the window of a confectioner's. The cost, according to rumour, has been set not far short of two thousand pounds, and the execution is likely to make Elkington and Company their name, if not their fortune.

And what does it show? Why, you know what, Vane. Lord Eglinton rewarded by the Queen of Beauty, and with a little phallic silver dart, while a defeated knight looks on.

'But the face of the Queen,' says Maclise, as we sip our Madeira, 'now who do you suppose the model for that would have been? Why, Lady Jane, one might have believed. Who else, indeed? Not so, however. Not so, I think. The face of the Queen is the face, I dare swear, of our Lady Frances Anne Vane-Tempest that was, the Marchioness of Londonderry.

'And the defeated knight? It looks very much to me, and I

took a close glance, I can tell you, there on the bench, and it was in bright sunlight, I swear, very much it looks like the 3rd Marquess of Londonderry in person. Now what would you make of that, I say?'

I am drifting away from my thoughts that day in Tunbridge Wells, as I walked amidst the puddles, intent on finding tobacco. I soon fell in, as it happened, with a fellow-spirit, and indeed a fellow-sufferer.

There in the dim cigar shop, stooping at the counter, and frowning down from under his great eyebrows, whom should I encounter but our poetical Alfred Tennyson, as mournful, as it turned out, and as much in need of a good smoke, and a confiding conversation, as I was myself.

He was then, as he is now, I gather, entirely infatuated with one of the Smallwood girls, but far too short of cash, or prospects, to marry, and thus contemplating the breaking off of all correspondence with the lady.

Of course, this real aspect of the matter was rather slow to emerge, and stayed out of sight until several pipes had been duly filled and puffed, and we had made a round of the whole town, and fetched up at his parents' house, where we occupied, alone after a brief salutation of the old couple, and a glass of port, an untidy, gloomy, smoke-redolent attic, the cave of making, as it were, in which the true state of our mutual feelings broke forth.

'So you have just married, Benjamin,' says Tennyson.

'And you are engaged, Alfred,' say I.

Then we nod, and smoke, and think for a while. Then he growls out, in between continuing puffs at his huge brier, several dispersed thoughts about the morals and the passions of the aristocracy in the vein of his kind hearts and coronets passage in *Lady Clara Vere de Vere*.

'Alfred,' I say, and with a slight hiccup, Vane, I may add, as we are a little drunk from imbibing brandy, as well as light-headed from the inhaling of tobacco, 'you are absolutely correct. Let me tell you the story – in strictest confidence, of course – of my shattered life.'

So I told him, Vane – in the way one does tell a comparative stranger, if a sympathetic one – the exact nature of my feelings about money, and about Mary Anne, and about you.

It took some time. The shadows grew longer as the sun went down, and the fire had to be stoked up more than once, and poked, like a difficult verse, with a slow, probing delicacy that he has.

'You did the right thing, Disraeli,' he said. 'It may feel wrong. But what you did was right.'

Then he reached into a drawer, and took out a sheaf of papers, and read me a wonderful long poem which he called the 'Morte d'Arthur', and which was really, I suppose, a personal elegy about his friend Hallam, but which I could read, or hear, politically, as concerning the Duke of Wellington, and the need for a new era.

'The old order changeth,' I remember him saying, 'yielding place to new.' After that, I didn't hear very much else. It seemed to me to sum up exactly what I had in mind about the state of England.

So I told him my plans for a novel, and how it had affected my own life, and my theme about the pressures of adultery, and the intermingling of the past and the present, and he sat there nodding away and told me that he had something of the same thing in mind for a long poem on the Arthurian legends, where the Round Table would be the symbol for the control of the passions, and by then we were both rather far gone in spirits and tobacco, I think, and I rose and swayed and said goodbye and promised to bring Mary Anne round, and went down the wooden stairs in a great clatter, and I hope I didn't wake up either of the older Tennysons, and was promptly out in the street again and away back through the darkness, and more rain, to the Kentish Hotel, and my sleeping, and very wonderfully unjealous and uncomplaining wife.

I HAVE HAD A WEEK to consider your letter. George Smythe stepped out of his carriage as we were on the point of leaving, and left me a whole packet of correspondence, largely financial, with your own lavender epistle tucked very discreetly away in the middle.

Alas, Mary Anne was not very pleased. She suspects nothing, I think, and yet her irritation at my receiving private letters through Smythe, albeit ones she believes to be political, is a little excessive.

So we drove through West London, and on to the country, and at length beyond the confines of normal civilisation, with my dear wife in a mood, and I thus in low spirits.

Mercifully, the Deepdene proved an instant reviver. The sight of those feathering cedars, and the avenues of limes, and the old, calm house there in its valley, with its totally exotic and unpredictable interior, was at once enough to raise our spirits.

We have been installed, I may say, in what Hope calls the oriental bedroom, where there are panels faced with water-colours of Constantinople and Athens, and one of a group of brigands decoratively posing amidst a circle of dismantled tents and, I think, rather disgruntled camels.

There are low couches, and stools with the legs of lions, and a quantity of stuffs – I know not what variety of silks and carpets and skins and so on – and even a small cache of scimitars and Arab shields in one corner.

The whole room brings out, so Mary Anne avers, my own oriental fashion, and my air of being a dilapidated sphinx. Indeed, there is already a small jaunty sphinx in the room, one made of jasper, and supporting a brass tray, and therein a low saucer on which we are invited to burn incense.

Well. The ambience is very conducive to relaxation, and I am currently sprawled on the sofa, caressing the mouth of a Nile alligator, and reflecting on what I must say.

There is time, fortunately. Mary Anne is out riding with Manners and his sister – we have quite a claque of the new generation here, I must tell you, with Baillie-Cochrane and Monckton Milnes to name but two – and I fancy her occupation, on returning for tea, will be studying Hope's marine grotto.

Yes, Vane, I shall be left alone for some hours. As indeed I am each day. The word has been passed round all the serving staff that Mr Disraeli is composing a new work of fiction, and must be left entirely undisturbed.

So that I hear the sound of tiptoeing, and of suppressed whispers, like a soft, restful cooing of doves, whenever I put my quill to the page.

And so to your letter. You ask me to come over to Ireland, so that, you say, 'we can talk'. I wonder. Can we talk? I am doubtful if we have ever been able to talk. That has been partly the trouble.

No. I shall not come over to Ireland. For one thing, I am much too busy. When I am not writing, or planning to, there are endless political conversations, and the future lines of our Parliamentary action are now becoming very clear.

I am developing what might be called a political philosophy. From an argument here with Hope, and an agreement there with Manners, and a touch of Smythe's raillery, when he comes down, which he does often, and a brush with Baillie-Cochrane's obstinacy, which is a useful whetstone, as it were, I am on the verge of reshaping the Tory party entirely in our own image.

I know exactly what has to be done. The days of Peel and his practicality are soon to be over. The country yearns for a principle. The long succession of governments working only by expedient is to come to an end.

So that I cannot come over to join you. I mean, I am doubtful if I could come, even if I wanted to. Or at least, not for another month, until Hope has thrown us out, and we make shift for Bradenham.

Should I come then? Should I squeeze in a lightning dash across the Irish Sea, and be in your arms for a brief space in the wake of October? No, Vane. I think not.

The Tournament is over. We have armed ourselves, and done our exercises. We have ridden at speed along the barrier, and broken lances on each other's breast. We have tumbled in sawdust, and had our wounds dressed in silk and tarragon.

The rest is history. The decline of romance into farce. The totting up of the cost, and the selling off of the armour. The boring grand opera of Lord Burgersh. Even the parody of Colonel Fane.

You missed all that in Russia. The men riding on donkeys, and the women made up in soot. The Knight of the Kettle in mortal combat with the Knight of the Coal Scuttle. And five thousand southern yokels laughing their heads off at the silliness of the past. A sad affair, Vane. As ours, perhaps.

Adulterous days. And adulterous knights. Behind the cushions, the morals of the Regency. Beyond the windows, though, the poverty of the poor.

I have been gathering evidence. The excellent Dr Guthrie, in his log-book, has been kind enough to supply me with details of the outbreak of typhus which he was called in to deal with on the Eglinton estate, only a year before the Tournament.

'In one village', he writes, in his dry, crimson hand, as though printing his characters in blood, 'there were five cases of the disease in one family. Two adults and four children were living in a cottage some eighteen feet by ten, and nine high. The accommodation was arranged as a single room, with a small flight of wooden steps leading up to a platform, filling half of the space, and serving as a bedroom. There one small boy, tossing on a bed with his head over the edge of the platform, fell out in a delirium, and broke his skull on a stone six feet below on the ground floor. The surface of this lower room was of pressed mud, and ankle-deep in water during rain. Outside the only window, there was a dump of rotting vegetable matter. The family diet was bread and potatoes, their clothing rags. These conditions were all very favourable for the development of typhus and acute rheumatism. I felt certain that rehousing these people in better cottages, well-drained, and airier, would greatly alleviate their sufferings, and prevent the outbreak, or at least the spreading, of these diseases. But Eglinton would not hear of change. The building costs, as I understand, would never be able to be defrayed by the obtainable sums of rent accruing.'

A shame and a scandal. And something that my new book, as my new party, will aim to change.

I shall not, however, discourse on the Eglinton Tournament, or make this theme the centre-piece in the canvas I mean to draw. The time is not ripe.

No, Vane. The Tournament is over. The Victorian age has begun. I shall curl up in bed, night after night, with my comfortable and entirely devoted Mary Anne. And you will retire to your several palaces, week after week, and year after year, with your ageing, although still vigorous, Charles.

And yet, am I entirely suited to the home life, and the stringent morality, of our modern times? We shall see. Some lack of concentration, I notice, is often apparent in me when I bend my mind to the virtues and the delights of a noble woman.

We had news yesterday, I think from Milnes, that Francis Smythe has died. I wonder if you remember? I used to spend some time at his dotty Palladian villa in Basildon.

A skinny, frail-moustachioed, rather petulant ninny, I always found the man. Clara Bolton's lover. Yes. You remember that, now don't you, Vane? I thought you would.

He came in after I – and goodness knows how many others – had left the exhausted field. A prissy, spindle-shanked and very county proposition for a lover. He regarded the order of baronets, I believe, as the premier one in the kingdom.

That, of course, was why he had Maclise paint him and his family in fifteenth-century dress, descending the stone spiral of some imaginary manor house. He with his great hulking lance and his glimmering armour. Henrietta with her vast breasts bursting the ermine, and a blue cloth over her arm.

It was quite the sensation of the Academy in '37. Maclise, of course, was Henrietta's lover. Why else the cupid's arrow, and the peacock's feathers, and the sporting puppies? It reeked like an allegory of what was going on.

I wonder how she is? Dear Henrietta. I doubt if she ever had much to satisfy her appetites from the formally fornicating Francis. I gathered from Clara that she once had to exert herself to the bone, as it were, to obtain some signs of life from our dusty baronet.

Well. Henrietta was never one for that. She always preferred to be the done-by rather than the doer, if you see what I mean.

I think I might send a letter of condolence to Basildon.

Indeed, I think that I really ought to. I might suggest that we meet. Over there. Or perhaps in London.

It's been a long time. Nearly ten years, I should say. After all, it was over by the time I first met you at Molly Blessington's, Vane, in '35. But then, things are never really over, now are they?

Or, if they are, it's hard to believe that they are. I mean, when someone says that they are. I wonder. Surely I must have told you before about Henrietta Sykes and me? I didn't?

Well, forgive me, Vane. She was a thick, succulent, suet-pudding of a young prostitute in those days. Very much the same type as yourself, my dear. Came from a country rectory or a manor house in Norfolk.

It gives me a stretched feeling in my breeches, it really does, just to think of what we used to do to each other. Used to, though. Oh, yes.

Have no fear, Vane. You have no rival now. Not yet, anyway. Or none except Mary Anne. My love to Charles. Tell him we need to talk about the new session, and soon, perhaps.

I have plans. He might care to sup with me at the Carlton some evening in November. Sound him out, and ask him to write. And my regards to you, my dear. My best regards.

After all, we shall meet in the course of the season. At the Duchess of Cambridge's ball, perhaps. And then, who knows? Nothing is ever entirely what it seems.